Offspring

A Novel

SANDEEP M. BHATNAGAR

SPEAKING TIGER

SPEAKING TIGER BOOKS LLP
125A, Ground Floor, Shahpur Jat,
New Delhi 110049

Published by Speaking Tiger Books 2021

ISBN: 978-93-5447-200-8
eISBN: 978-93-5447-201-5

10 9 8 7 6 5 4 3 2 1

Typeset in ArnhemFine Regular by SÜRYA, New Delhi
Printed at Shree Maitrey Printech Pvt. Ltd., Noida

Sandeep M. Bhatnagar is the son of Late Meem Meem Rajinder, a celebrated Urdu fiction writer. He joined the IRS (Customs & Central Excise) in 1984 and is associated with numerous key reforms in the realm of indirect taxes—Customs, Central Excise & GST. Sandeep superannuated in August 2021 from the post of Member, Central Board of Indirect Taxes & Customs, Government of India. He is an awardee of the Presidential Award for specially meritorious service.

Offspring is based on Sandeep's personal experience and close interaction with immigrants when he was working in the Consulate General of India at New York. Sandeep resides in Delhi with his wife, Shalini. He has two children, Sanchit and Ashima.

To my dear parents,
Chachaji Dr Vijay Mohan Bhatnagar (Vimto),
Shalini, Sanchit and Sana

Your offspring shall be like the dust of the earth, and you shall spread abroad to the west and to the east and to the north and to the south, and in you and your offspring shall all the families of the earth be blessed.

—*Genesis 28:14*

PROLOGUE

Glendale, Ontario: 1991

The evening shadows deepen as I thumb through photographs of loved ones smiling through the ages. I softly caress their faded, grainy faces and succumb to the flash flood of joyful memories—my first meeting with Jenny, the love we shared walking hand in hand along the streets of Sydney and Paris, the fruition of our romance in Glendale, the ecstatic celebration of festivals with Baoji, Ma and Bhai back in Ambala. Then, as always, I pray I did not commit the sin of breaking my family and, when my time comes, someone in the land of my birth knows that Rohan—the younger son of Baoji and Ma, brother of Bhai, and husband of Jenny—is no more.

Ambala, Punjab: 1905–1918

Growing up in Ambala was interesting as I made sure my friends were in awe of me. I engineered this by fearlessly entering the fortified British cantonment to meet make-believe British friends though I actually met Baoji—my father—an accounts clerk with the British Commandant. I often reinforced this impression by energetically saluting uniformed soldiers on horseback till I elicited, what my friends believed, a familiar nod.

We lived in a modest, indifferently whitewashed, two-bedroom house in Bengali Mohalla. The house had a small living room and an even smaller kitchen. Initially a rental, Baoji purchased it at some stage. Its unkempt backyard housed a grassy patch with numerous weeds and a tall guava tree. I spent a substantial part of my childhood on its branches for it bore the most delicious fruit—bright yellow on the outside, dark red inside—each bite sweeter than honey. It was also the one place Ma could not catch me to punish me for some mischief.

Bhai, my brother who was seven years older to me, was the neighbourhood darling. He was quite different. While boys his age bunked school and stole fruit and other stuff from street sellers, Bhai focused on academics. Maybe this was because Baoji, who secretly greatly admired the Crown, strictly enforced his imagined brand of 'British discipline', and being the firstborn, Bhai got the brunt of it. Each child of our neighbourhood was invariably reprimanded by a parent, claiming wistfully, 'I wish you were like Bhai'. In fact, everyone called him Bhai and I am sure few knew his real name, Madan Lal. Growing up, I often overheard our neighbours comment how different I was from him, which was no compliment.

Our neighbourhood was like a large extended family. The children played all day amongst stray cows, dogs and sometimes monkeys, while the women sat on cots under the shade of a large peepal tree next to a waterless well, drank tea, cut vegetables and animatedly discussed upcoming weddings and festivals. We freely entered each other's houses, respectfully addressing the older children as brothers and sisters and the adults as uncles and aunts. Boys took up ancestral occupations while girls married early within the community. Life was slow paced, simple and everyone was by and large content: a person would be born, grow up, and pass on in the same neighbourhood.

Professor Hardayal's entry into B.D. High School was a welcome change to a student body bored of the routine. I never suspected the chaos he would cause in my life.

Happily working at the Australian Academy of Sciences in Sydney, Professor Hardayal decided to come back to Ambala to tend to his aged mother. At the slightest provocation—a misstep on the broken floor, a piece of chalk breaking, his chair wobbling, just about anything—he would instantly embark on a nostalgic trip to Australia. Speaking as if he had spent a lifetime there, he would passionately relive his Sydney sojourn and severely criticize everything Indian. This went on until the dismissal bell brought him back to reality. The entertainment he provided made his class most popular.

I soon became the professor's favourite because I could somehow easily remember complex chemical formulae while others struggled. This made my classmates prompt me to entice him to recall his memories of Australia, allowing backbenchers to escape from a window, confident the good professor would not notice.

One day, as I raised my hand yet again to answer a question, Professor Hardayal suddenly lost his temper. 'It is always only you while everybody else is sleeping.'

His face turned red and the vein on his forehead throbbed wildly as he continued. 'My life's greatest tragedy is to be here, surrounded by you dullards, when I could have been with Nobel Prize winners in Australia. All you dumb children should be locked up in jail! Only Rohan has merit and you will spoil him too, but I will make sure this does not happen. I will send him to Australia, far from your bad influence!'

The professor began gathering his books, as we all mutely watched him struggle to keep his anger in check. He stomped out of the classroom a good twenty minutes before time.

Years down the line, I would often think back on the exact moment I innocently raised my hand and wonder how different my life would have been had I not done so.

One day after recess, Professor Hardayal beckoned me to the staff room. Familiar with his idiosyncrasies and adept at humouring him, I followed him in. The staff room was unoccupied and he summoned Ramu, the peon, for tea before settling in an armchair, gesturing to me to sit by his side. I now noticed he was holding a brown envelope. He opened it carefully and held a sheet of paper out to me. It was a letter bearing a floral insignia inscribed with the words: 'Australian Academy of Sciences'.

Bewildered, I looked at Professor Hardayal for a hint and he smiled indulgently. 'I have always believed that you are capable of achieving great things. So, I sent your final results to the Academy. They accept international students for a five-year undergraduate programme and a bright future is assured to those who complete it. You know, they hold me in high esteem and Professor Hubertson, who chairs the Admission Committee, is a good friend. This is his reply. He has cleared you for admission and I want you to accept this offer and turn your life around.'

Professor Hardayal's words left me dumbstruck and out of breath. Trying to make sense of it all, I continued to blankly pore over the admission letter. Why, I had so far not even stepped outside Ambala! Even as I struggled to grasp what he had just told me, it was clear that Professor Hardayal had indeed lost his mind.

He continued, completely ignoring me. 'There is no expense as the Academy will pay fare and boarding.'

'But Professor,' I finally stuttered. 'How can I go so far?'

'Don't worry at all, son,' the professor assured kindly. 'Leave everything to me. Just take these papers home to read. I will come over tomorrow to discuss this with Baoji.'

'But Professor...' I struggled to reason as I imagined Baoji's reaction upon hearing this; he frowned upon fanciful ideas, his modest aspiration extending to Bhai and I getting petty government jobs. I could well see him red-faced, turning both Professor Hardayal and me out of the house. I urgently pleaded again. 'Wait, Professor. Please don't do this. Baoji will be very angry. You know we cannot afford this.'

'What rubbish,' he chided. 'I just told you it's all paid for. Leave it to me to convince Baoji.'

'But Professor,' I implored, 'Baoji will never agree. I too don't want to go. I will look for a government job when the time comes.'

My protests flustered Professor Hardayal and he spoke sharply. 'Do you even know what you are saying? Thousands apply to this programme and you are so fortunate to be accepted because of my recommendation. It will change your life! Tell Baoji I will be at your house tomorrow at 6 p.m.'

Summarily dismissed, I left in a daze, tightly clutching the envelope which seemed to burn my hands. In the classroom I quickly hid it in my bag, trying to pay attention but my mind was in a whirl. Having been at the receiving end of Baoji's anger time and again, I feared the worst when Professor Hardayal met him.

Back home, I hid the envelope under my mattress and went out to play cricket, but my heart was not in it and I returned home earlier than usual. Once the coast was clear, I shut the bedroom door and took out the envelope. The promise of a foreign land was so enchanting that my guard slipped and Bhai entered as I hastily slid the envelope behind my back.

'What are you hiding?'

'Nothing at all, Bhai.'

'Your report card? Don't worry if you have done badly, I will save you from Baoji.'

'Won't get it for another week and you know I will top the class.'

'Then, what is it?'

'Nothing really, just something the crazy Professor gave me.'

'OK. But don't come to me later if you are in trouble.'

Bhai's words made me think and I approached him with the envelope hesitantly.

'I have been accepted at the Australian Academy of

Sciences in Sydney because Professor Hardayal posted my results without even telling me. I told him I am not interested, but he insists he will discuss this tomorrow with Baoji. And he will think I planned this and be very angry. I just don't know what to do!'

Bhai silently took the envelope from me while I quietly sat beside him. He opened it carefully and took out few brochures and the covering letter that the professor had shown me. It was from a Professor Hubertson and was addressed to me—'Rohan Lal c/o Professor Hardayal'.

Bhai began reading even as I explained in a low voice that Professor Huberston was Professor Hardayal's friend. Indeed, the letter confirmed my admission to the undergraduate course in chemistry with full tuition waiver and free boarding. Also, as a special case, the Academy was bearing my sea fare. Bhai put down the letter with a big smile.

'Why, Rohan, this is wonderful news indeed!'

'But I don't want to go.'

'What will you do here? This will help you get a fine job upon your return.'

'I don't want to go. It is too far away.'

I guess I looked vulnerable because Bhai put his hand on my shoulder and reassured me. 'Don't worry. We will discuss this with Baoji and he will take the right decision. I understand you are anxious, but this may well be a turning point of your life.'

'You talk to Baoji. Also, tell him Professor Hardayal will come tomorrow evening.'

'Come on, you can't hide from Baoji forever. Let us go together.'

After some cajoling I followed Bhai to Baoji's bedroom, all the time staying a safe distance behind him. Baoji was reading a newspaper and Ma sat by his side cutting vegetables. Bhai began, 'Baoji, I want to show you something.'

'Tell me,' Baoji replied, keeping his newspaper aside. Then looking at me, he added, 'I hope Rohan has not got into trouble again.'

Bhai handed him Professor Hubertson's letter. 'Baoji, Professor Hardayal applied for Rohan's admission in Sydney, Australia, without telling him. This is the admission letter.' I hung my head, embarrassed.

'Australia?' Ma inquired, immediately stopping work.

'Yes, Ma,' Bhai explained, while Baoji read the letter silently. 'They are paying fare, tuition, and boarding. It is an excellent opportunity.'

'Have you gone mad?' Ma snapped. 'How can a child go so far? Do you even know where Australia is?'

'Hush. Let me read,' Baoji commanded and Ma became quiet. I took this opportunity to weakly mutter to no one in particular that all this was Professor Hardayal's fault, but Baoji glared at me and I too fell silent.

Baoji read and re-read the letter carefully before folding it neatly and silently handing it back to Bhai. Then, looking at me, he spoke in a measured tone. 'It is creditable to be accepted by a prestigious university, but foreign studies are not for us. You are also too young to travel abroad. They say there is no expense, but I know there will be heavy expenditure that we cannot afford. So, first thing tomorrow, tell Professor Hardayal we are not interested and return this to him with thanks.'

I heaved a sigh of relief, but Bhai protested. 'Baoji, this letter confirms, unambiguously, that everything is paid for. This is a golden opportunity and a foreign degree will ensure a good job.'

Baoji had never appreciated anyone questioning his verdicts and this time was no different. He retorted agitatedly, 'What do *you* know? My decision is final, no more arguments!' He went back to reading the newspaper, unaffected. Bhai looked pleadingly at Ma, but she was obviously happy with Baoji's decision. Bhai exited the room upset and I followed suit, silently thanking God for His mercy.

Entering our room, I suddenly remembered Professor Hardayal was coming over the next day and turned to Bhai. 'What about Professor Hardayal?'

'What about him?' Bhai snapped.

'Well, you did not tell Baoji he is coming tomorrow.'

Still cheesed off, Bhai replied, 'You should have told him. Here, take this and deal with it.'

Thrusting the envelope into my hands he turned his back on me. Unsure of how to handle the impending disaster, I retreated quietly; my relief at escaping Baoji's wrath had been short lived.

As Bhai dozed peacefully, I lay awake, petrified, visualizing Baoji angrily turning away Professor Hardayal. My infrequent snatches of sleep were punctuated by visions of a livid Baoji strangling Professor Hardayal lying on the floor gasping for breath, weakly waving my admission form. As night progressed, I dreamt of getting evicted from home by Baoji.

I woke up drenched in cold sweats and sheer desperation led me to seek divine intervention for deliverance from my predicament. I had acquired a rudimentary knowledge of relevant Gods from Ma and so prayed earnestly till I drifted off.

Bhai shook me awake the next morning. 'Wake up! Are you fine? Get up, you are having a nightmare.'

'What happened, Bhai?' I asked groggily but then quickly came to my senses remembering Professor Hardayal's impending visit.

'You were mumbling so much in your sleep.'

'Really, what was I saying?'

'It was mostly incomprehensible, but you kept muttering "Shiva".'

I sheepishly remembered praying but felt relieved I had not dreamed that part.

As I was about to go freshen up, Bhai asked, 'Who is Shiva?'

'No one, Bhai, I don't remember anything. I was sleeping soundly.'

'No, you were not. You were obviously disturbed.'

I hesitated before replying. 'Well, Professor Hardayal is coming to meet Baoji so I thought it would not hurt to remember God Shiva.'

'Whose death or destruction were you praying for? Professor Hardayal's?'

I looked at him incredulously. 'What do you mean? Don't you understand? I prayed to God Shiva for good luck.'

'Are you nuts? Don't tell me you don't know your Gods. Shiva is the God of Death, the Destroyer.'

Bhai was right. Of course, it was Ganesha the Elephant God, Shiva's child, who removed obstacles and brought good luck! I had mixed up my Gods! I collapsed on my bed, amidst Bhai's laughter, beating myself over praying all night to the wrong God!

Time passed agonizingly slowly. I was a nervous wreck by late afternoon. I quietly left home, all the time praying feverishly, this time to Lord Ganesha, to save me from this crisis.

After walking aimlessly for a bit, I decided to secretly observe Professor Hardayal's visit from a safe distance. Baoji usually calmed after about an hour of an aggravation.

Retracing my steps, I carefully choose a vantage spot behind the bushes next to a teashop, about a hundred feet from home. Mosquitoes readily attacked me, but I did not forsake my vigil. Sure enough, Professor Hardayal, rather nattily dressed, soon appeared at the doorstep and knocked. As my heart thumped in my ears, the door opened and shut solidly behind him.

I gave Professor Hardayal's inglorious exit ten minutes at most, five for niceties and five for Baoji's explosion. Anytime now, anytime, I thought, the door would burst open and Professor Hardayal would stomp off furiously, planning an evil end for me. But even as dusk fell everything remained ominously silent.

With each passing moment I grew more sure that Baoji had lost control and killed the professor. After what felt like hours, the door opened and Professor Hardayal came out, seemingly untouched, along with Baoji and they began walking towards me. Nonplussed, I swiftly lay on the ground, perfectly concealed. They stopped at the teashop, barely a few feet away from where I lay when I heard Baoji. 'Here is some paan. You will like it very much.'

'Thank you,' replied Professor Hardayal. 'I must go now.'

Puzzled at the anticlimax, I lay still, silently cursing the blood-sucking mosquitoes but Baoji and Professor Hardayal appeared to be in no hurry to part. Finally, Professor Hardayal thanked Baoji and began walking away and I heaved a sigh of relief now that my ordeal was over.

Just as the professor passed by my hideout, he unknowingly spit the gooey paan straight onto my head!

After the coast cleared I dusted myself, cleaned the mess on my head and examined the mosquito bites all over me. Though confused at the camaraderie I had just witnessed, I decided it was safe to return home.

I had almost crossed the living room when Baoji stopped me. 'Rohan, come here.'

'Yes, Baoji,' I replied shakily; he sounded stern and I tensed. Just then Ma came from the kitchen and she too appeared angry. It was clear I was in deep trouble regardless of what I had observed earlier.

'Sit down, son,' said Baoji, but I kept standing; from past experience I knew his deportment could be misleading and I was prepared to flee at the slightest hint of violence.

'Professor Hardayal just came over and explained how he had applied for your admission without your knowledge.'

'Yes Baoji. I don't want to go.'

'He says it is an excellent opportunity.'

'I don't trust him, Baoji. Nobody likes him at school. I don't want to go.'

'What do you mean? Is this any way to talk about your teacher?' Baoji retorted angrily.

'I don't want to go,' I muttered weakly.

'What do you mean you don't want to go? Stop repeating the same thing like a parrot. You think you can decide for yourself?'

Bhai and Ma stood as silent observers while Baoji continued to scold me. 'Only English lords and Indian princes study in foreign lands and here you are, a good-for-nothing fellow getting this golden opportunity and throwing it away. What will you do here? Are there jobs here? You will become a beggar, or worse, a criminal and end up in prison!'

Thankfully Ma intervened to plead my case. 'He is too young. He has not even stepped outside Ambala yet.'

Baoji instantly turned on her. 'Will you keep him by your side all his life? This opportunity is a godsend. He will be back before you know it. He will live like a king!'

Ma knew better than to argue when Baoji was in this mood. He continued, 'Only Madan here has the good sense to support my decision. My mind is made. We cannot miss this excellent opportunity. I will let Professor Hardayal know.'

Having made his grand announcement, Baoji dismissed me with an indifferent wave of his hand. Ma silently sat next to him. I retreated. Even in my wildest imagination I had not expected Baoji to support Professor Hardayal's silly plan, but here he was endorsing it!

Bhai came up to me as I sat on my bed. 'Don't worry, Rohan. I genuinely feel this is the best decision for you. You will thoroughly enjoy the experience. You will even get to meet royalty abroad!'

Listening to Bhai, I began imagining myself in a wonderland and in the company of royalty. Why, I could live with that! Transported to an enticing world, I saw myself in the midst of new friends, the cream of society, enjoying the rich treats they piled on me. Then, all of a sudden, I remembered what was nagging me: what made Baoji change his mind?

'Bhai, what did Professor say to Baoji? I was expecting fireworks and to be thrown out of the house but now Baoji is letting me go abroad!'

'Well, it surprised me too, but when Professor Hardayal began recounting his wonderful experiences in Australia, I sensed Baoji was getting hooked. Then, the professor explained about the scholarship. Baoji remarked that no one in our family had ever left Ambala and Ma said that she had heard criminals are sent to Australia. The professor patiently explained that the place was perfectly safe. He also said that given the current disturbed political situation you might find it difficult to find a job without this programme.

'Baoji said that parents want the best for children, even if that means bearing the pain of separation and so he would consider the offer seriously. Professor Hardayal sounded relieved and told us that we had a week to decide. I thought Baoji would take some time with the decision, but it seems his mind is made.'

I was too dazed to respond. So far, I had never spent even a night away from home. How would I live so far away? That night, I dreamt of a long sea voyage, filled with silvery moonlit nights and golden sunrises. I reached a fabulous place where I moved about with rich friends, in horse-drawn chariots and everybody addressed me as 'Prince Rohan'.

Despite Ma's objection, Baoji conveyed his concurrence to Professor Hardayal within the week. Ma continued to voice her reservations for a few days, but once Baoji convinced her that it was for my benefit, she kept her concerns to herself.

The news spread like wildfire; Baoji made it seem as if it had been his plan all along to send his son to study abroad. I became an instant celebrity at school, in the neighbourhood and in all of Ambala. At a time when adults rarely stepped out of the city, I was the boy going abroad!

I was to leave for Australia in about eight months and Bhai and Professor Hardayal teamed up to attend to paper work. I completed high school and could do as I liked, but as most of my friends had begun work, I mostly stayed home which wasn't all that bad for Baoji was now much more indulgent. Thus, I became privy to many discussions. I came to know that Bhai was so far unemployed as he didn't want to work outside Ambala and leave Baoji and Ma alone. Baoji and Ma were also anxious to get Bhai married before I left, but that too depended on his employment status. It seemed too rushed until I realized that a few of his friends were already married and one even had a child. Bursting with excitement, I rushed to Bhai to tell him, but he declined to discuss it.

Despite his excellent academic record, Bhai's job hunt had been going on for nearly two years. Every day he would faithfully read each employment advertisement in the newspaper while also dealing with my admission formalities. I often sat by his side as he filled my forms meticulously, carefully sealed them in an envelope, and then wrote the address in his best possible handwriting. Only upon my insistence would he trust me to take the envelope to the Commandant's office for dispatch. Considering the complicated route—Ambala to Delhi to Calcutta to Rangoon to Singapore to Sydney—it was truly a wonder the documents reached the Academy.

One evening when I mustered the courage to ask Bhai about his marriage plans, he replied plainly. 'Marriage is an alliance between two families. Sure, I want happiness, for myself and for the girl I marry, but our families too must be happy.'

'But Bhai, how can anyone be happy with a stranger?'

'Are you saying Ma and Baoji are not happy? This is how it has always been and people learn to love each other.'

'You are speaking like Baoji! Tell me frankly, will you not be happier with Seema, who you know since you both were children? My friends and I always see her looking out for you and think she loves you.'

Bhai froze and I cringed, fearing I had crossed a line. After a few seconds, he whispered, sternly. 'Make sure you don't repeat this to anyone. Caution your friends too. If a word of this spreads, poor Seema will be a spinster all her life.'

'This is ridiculous! If you like her too why can't you marry her?'

'We are not in England where boys and girls themselves

decide whom they want to marry. She is from a different caste and neither her family nor Baoji will agree to our marriage.'

Bhai refused to discuss the matter anymore. As I watched him work late into the night, a part of me felt sad to know that he was readily forsaking his happiness for Baoji and Ma but the other felt proud.

An unexpected development was that Professor Hardayal decided to tutor me. Had he spoken to me, I may have somehow wriggled out, but he directly obtained Baoji's concurrence. Both Baoji and Bhai felt indebted, but I knew he was only ensuring that I did not embarrass him at the Academy. So, he gave me a one-hour lesson on alternate days. He was far more formidable in close proximity and the prospect filled with me with terror, but I had no option.

The routine was interspersed with moments of excitement, like when I got mail from the Academy, or Bhai's job quest showed signs of fruition, and prominent British institutions, such as the Imperial Bank, called him for an interview.

One evening Baoji announced at dinner that he and Ma had to urgently visit Sangrur, a small town about five hours by bus, to meet a close friend, Master Prasad. Bhai later told me he had never heard of this 'close friend' and since he was preoccupied with his approaching interview, he didn't pay it much heed.

Next morning Bhai saw them off at the bus stop and upon their return, later that night, Baoji and Ma immediately retired. It was only the following morning when Baoji summoned us that the reason for their mysterious visit was revealed.

Baoji sat in his favorite chair, drinking tea, next to Ma. After we said Namaste, Bhai asked, 'Baoji, you called?'

Bhai sat down and I followed suit. Ma gave him a glowing smile. It was evident something was unusual. Then Baoji explained. 'You must be wondering about our visit to Sangrur. Well, we met Master Prasad's family and your Ma liked his eldest daughter a lot. She is the perfect match for you and will fit well into our family. I have given my word that you will marry her.'

I glanced at Bhai who instantly froze and stared at Baoji who had reverted to his newspaper. Bhai slowly turned to Ma, who took a sweet from a packet by her side and offered it to him with an encouraging smile. 'Congratulations! Here, have something sweet.' Still dazed, he took the sweet from Ma and turned to Baoji. 'But Baoji...'

Baoji was back in his element. Lowering the newspaper only slightly he glowered and said sharply. 'What "but"? This is a heaven-sent match and they are prepared to wait till you get a job. What more can be expected? The family is highly respected in our community.'

Bhai had never reacted to Baoji and this time was no different. He got up slowly to leave but I could not hold myself back any longer. 'But Baoji, shouldn't Bhai decide whom to marry?'

Baoji was irate. 'What nonsense! Who ever heard such things? Your Ma and I have made a decision and that is final. Do you doubt for a moment that we do not know what is good for Bhai? And who taught you to argue with your elders? Go do your work!'

Bhai and I quietly retreated to our room. He shared the piece of sweet he was still holding with me. Between munches Bhai conceded that he should have suspected something when he saw Pandit Hari Shankar, an irritant reviled by us all for strictly policing the mango trees in the temple compound but a trusted matchmaker, in their bus. He still couldn't believe it: he was getting married!

Ma celebrated the news by distributing sweets amongst neighbours and relatives who immediately scored off Bhai's name from their lists of eligible bachelors. If Bhai failed to secure a job he would most likely remain a bachelor, besides being responsible for the family's ignominy. Thus, his job search took on a new urgency.

Baoji had brought no photograph so we had no idea of how Bhai's bride-to-be looked. It would have been considered disrespectful for Bhai to seek details, so I became his source of information, exacting my pound of flesh before revealing small nuggets elicited from Ma.

We got to know that Bhai was promised to Hema, eldest of seven daughters and one son of Master Prasad, a school teacher who was 'respectable', a euphemism for poor. Hema was 'homely', which I understood translated to 'ordinary looking' and proficient in household chores.

As per convention, no contact was possible between the boy and girl until the day of the wedding, so normalcy was soon restored. Bhai began preparing hard for his interview and, at times, appeared to forget about his impending marriage.

My departure date was finally fixed for two months later and Baoji and Ma desperately prayed for Bhai to get a job so he could marry before I left. Finally, when it appeared this was unlikely in the available short time, Baoji deemed it was important that I at least meet my future sister-in-law and Bhai would accompany me. This was rather unconventional, for tradition dictated that the boy and girl could not meet before marriage but Bhai did not complain.

Thus, one Sunday morning Bhai and I boarded the bus to Sangrur; I was thoroughly enjoying the special treatment I was getting while Bhai struggled to suppress his excitement. Baoji's parting words to me were: 'Mind you, don't speak or eat too much'. To Bhai he said, 'Don't forget, I have given my word'.

The bus steadily ate up the dusty miles. The monotony broke every time the bus stopped at a new village. Finally, after about four hours, the conductor yelled, 'Reaching main road, Sangrur, in five minutes,' and shook us out of our reverie.

The desolate scenery soon began filling up with houses on either side and we neared a huge gateway.

'Look, Bhai, it says, "Sangrur". We have reached.'

I hastily pulled out our bag and kept it on my lap; this contained fresh sweets for Master Prasad and a saree for Hema especially sent by Ma. Our bus barely slowed upon entering the city gate and we were suddenly in a busy market place packed with people, bicycles, horse drawn carts, and numerous vegetable and fruit vendors. Incessantly sounding the horn by pressing and releasing a small rubber ball-like contraption, the driver expertly guided the bus through the teeming crowds. All this while, the conductor played his part to perfection: hanging by the door of the bus, banging a stone against the side and shouting epithets if anyone dared impede his charge. Finally, we screeched to a halt in a small clearing. We had reached Sangrur, capital of the State of Jind.

I hoisted my bag on my shoulder and encouraged Bhai. 'Come on, I am hungry and Master Prasad would surely have a feast prepared for his son-in-law.'

'Hush!' Bhai whispered sternly. 'People may know him.'

We got off the bus among the milling crowd but nobody stepped forward to meet us. Just then, Bhai spotted a thin boy scrutinizing the crowd. 'Look, he seems to be looking for somebody.'

'Maybe this is your brother-in-law? Let us ask him.'

'Don't be silly. We can't just ask someone if he is here for us.'

'And why not? You want to wait here all day?'

Our dilemma was resolved when the boy began walking towards us, pulling his bicycle along.

The boy placed his bicycle on its stand and approached us with folded hands. 'Namaste. Are you visiting Master Prasad?'

'Yes,' Bhai replied. 'I am Madan and this is Rohan, my brother.'

'I am Kishan. Master Prasad is my father.'

'It is really nice to meet you, Kishan.'

'Everyone at home is very excited and I am glad to be the first to meet you. Baoji said you are returning by evening?'

'Yes, our bus departs at 5 p.m.'

'Baoji has sent a tonga. Here, let me take your bag, Rohan, and we can start for home right away.'

As we boarded the finest chariot in Sangrur, Kishan rode beside us on his bicycle.

Our tonga wound its way through various lanes with Kishan dishing out facts about the various landmarks on our way.

After a few minutes he declared, 'My house is in the next alley,' and sped ahead, stopping next to a tall person who was undoubtedly Master Prasad.

As we halted, we heard a few neighbourhood ladies excitedly whisper about 'the new son-in-law'.

'Here we are, Sirs,' said the tonga owner, getting down with a flourish and holding the reins to steady his horse. 'Masterji, I have brought your guests. I am sure they will have no complaints.'

'Yes, yes,' Master Prasad replied, stepping forward. 'I can always depend upon you. Kishan will give you tea.' Then he greeted us with folded hands. 'Welcome, sons. I hope you had a comfortable journey.'

'Yes, Sir,' Bhai replied politely, getting down and touching his feet and I followed suit. 'I am Madan and this is Rohan.'

'You are just like in the photograph Baoji showed us. So, Rohan, I hear you are going abroad. Baoji is proud of you.'

'Thank you, Sir.'

We sat in the living room and after a brief awkward silence, Master Prasad asked, 'What would you like to drink?'

'We are fine, Sir,' Bhai replied tentatively and handed over the sweets and gifts we had brought for their family.

'Your Baoji is too kind. Please convey our thanks to him. Also, please feel at home. You should freshen up first.'

Kishan led us to a bathroom and Bhai entered to wash away the dust and grime of the journey, coming out seemingly transformed, no longer diffident and unsure. It was my turn next and when I returned to the living room, Bhai was talking to Master and Mrs Prasad freely.

'We are happy you and Rohan could visit us, even if only for a few hours,'Master Prasad was saying.

Kishan brought us fresh juice and Master Prasad continued, 'You should meet the others. As you would know, Hema is the eldest and Kishan is fourth in line. Kishan, please ask your sisters to join us.'

With that, my confidence left the room and I nervously focused on my shoes. Bhai seemed to sit up straighter and admire a wall painting just as the curtain moved and a few girls entered the room.

To this day, I cannot recall what exactly followed. I remember the curtain rustling and three young girls coming in. Master Prasad introduced them as 'Hema, Rajan and Doll.' I had barely glanced at them when almost immediately a few more girls entered the room. Master Prasad continued reciting their names. The troupe sat all around and silently stared at us, barring the sporadic giggles. Master Prasad tried to initiate conversation, even asking the youngest to sing, but she would just not stop blushing. A heavy silence descended and Bhai again found refuge admiring the painting, which led Master Prasad to comment, 'Hema painted this. She is a very good artist.'

'I agree, Sir,' Bhai replied shakily. 'It is excellent'.

His polite remark was somehow extremely amusing to the younger elements of the babble, who began giggling uncontrollably. Master Prasad's stern gaze made it worse and almost dissolving into hysterical laughter, they ran out of the room one after the other.

The sudden exodus left Master and Mrs Prasad acutely embarrassed as the latter excused herself to admonish the girls in hushed tones in an attempt to restore some semblance of order.

Master Prasad was apologetic. 'The girls are excited, they meant no disrespect.'

Bhai was back to his confident self. 'We understand, Sir.'

'Well, it is already 2 p.m., let us have lunch.' Master Prasad led us to an alcove and as we ate, Mrs Prasad tried to ascertain Bhai's likes and dislikes, proudly claiming Hema's culinary prowess over every dish he mentioned. We retired to the living room after lunch.

Time had flown and it was now 4 p.m. Master Prasad left to inquire about the arrangements to take us to the bus stop. Bhai and I were alone for the first time since coming to Sangrur and I made the most out of it. 'Did you see her?'

'What do you mean?' Bhai whispered back.

'I am not sure which of Master Prasad's daughters is your bride-to-be.'

'To tell you the truth even I don't know.'

'I think she was the old one in the blue saree.'

'Old! What do you mean "old"? She is four years younger than me.'

'I mean the eldest one.'

'I think she was the one who brought us dessert.'

'No, Master Prasad called her by another name. I still feel she was the one in blue.'

'But how can we know for sure? *I* definitely cannot ask so you think of something. And do it quickly, we are about to leave.'

We conspired an excellent plan. I would tell Kishan that I wanted to meet my sister-in-law before leaving; hopefully she would come out alone this time. But before I could get to execute my plan, Master and Mrs Prasad came back to the room. As per custom, Mrs Prasad placed a vermilion mark and few rice kernels, first on Bhai's forehead and then mine. Then Master Prasad gave Bhai a packet of sweets and some shirt fabric. 'These are for Baoji and Ma.'

We were escorted out and Kishan placed our bag back on the tonga as we thanked Master and Mrs Prasad for their hospitality. Just then, the window curtain quivered. Bhai was sure his Hema was behind it.

As we left Sangrur behind, Bhai looked somber not having a clue how his fiancée looked. I too felt bad for him and told him my theory. 'Is it not strange that the entire day nobody told us who Hema was? I am sure she has a squint or pockmarks and Master Prasad didn't want you to reject her so he cleverly made his girls come all together to confuse us.'

My clever explanation got me a clip on the head and I made no more quips. It was clear our trip had been an unqualified disaster.

An excited Ma welcomed us home. It was late and we went straight to bed, brushing aside Ma's questions. We could not have ignored Baoji, but thankfully he had retired.

I awoke the next morning to find Bhai and Baoji gone for some work. Ma instantly cornered me, asked questions and complained bitterly about my cryptic replies. She prodded, 'At least tell me did your Bhai like Hema?'

'Come on, Ma,' I replied. 'Leave me alone. I am tired.'

'Well, I'll ask Madan,' she said, a little hurt by my brusqueness.

'OK do that,' I replied and went to my room realizing just then that we would appear mighty foolish if anyone learned that neither Bhai nor I had a clue about Hema. I stepped out to find Bhai and warn him to keep this a secret.

Baoji was surprisingly most affected by my imminent departure, which was a revelation for he prided himself on being a disciplinarian and was never one to display emotion. As the day of parting drew nearer, I often chanced upon him in my room. He would pretend to be searching for something and exit quickly. At times, late at night, while I feigned deep sleep, he would tip toe in to look at me before softly running his fingers through my hair. I so wished to hug him tight, but I respected him too much to destroy the image he had created. Outwardly so proud of me, he seemed to age overnight in sorrow. Once I overheard him confess to Ma: 'He is going so far, I fear I will die without seeing him again.'

Ma, too, was grieving but she kept her feelings hidden. Bhai pretended to be happy about getting rid of me, but I knew he would miss me the most. During the days leading up to my departure, our house had a strange feel about it. Each person got unduly busy in preparing for my departure, but no one spoke openly about it.

I had mixed feelings: excitement coupled with the fear of leaving behind the familiar. I often tried to visualize my new life, but this soon became a frightening exercise thanks to the many 'safety rules' Baoji daily drilled into me. These safety rules included sewing money in an inner vest pocket to keep it, safe from crooks; not talking to strangers who would forcibly convert me to Christianity; and not being outdoors after dusk to avoid drunkards and murderers and, for some reason, my instant internment.

One particular safety rule warned me to stay away from Australian girls. Unlike with his other rules, Baoji offered no explanation for this one, so naturally I asked him how exactly this was unsafe. I knew I was in trouble the instant the question left my mouth. His eyes almost popped out in anger and I was grilled for the next few minutes for already being disrespectful. I overheard later that this rule was especially included to counteract Baoji and Ma's greatest fear—of me settling abroad. Baoji repeated his safety rules so often they made me a nervous wreck till I stopped taking them seriously.

Time flew once my tickets arrived and Professor Hardayal declared that I was fully prepared and stopped tutoring me. It felt good being at home; I guess I wanted to cling to my family for as long as possible.

The strain of unemployment was now telling on Bhai especially as Master Prasad began inquiring about it every week, compelling Baoji to give evasive but hopeful replies. So, I began helping him. Just as I sealed one more job application, I heard Ma call, 'Rohan, here is a letter for Bhai.'

I rushed to Ma as Bhai, who had just entered, grabbed the envelope from her. It was from the Imperial Bank. Mouthing a silent prayer, he opened it and read aloud: 'We are pleased to offer you the position of Accountant at the salary of 50 rupees per month.' As I leaped to hug him, Bhai slowly sank on a chair and looking at Ma, who had not fully comprehended, said simply. 'Ma, I have got a job.'

'Really, son!' Ma embraced Bhai. She rushed to her kitchen temple and came back with some sweetened curd, giving Bhai and me a spoonful each. 'Son, I am so happy! Now quickly go give this happy news to your Baoji.'

Carefully pocketing the appointment letter, Bhai rushed out. I followed close behind. We had been waiting so long for this day! Laughing and shouting gleefully we practically ran all the way to Baoji's office. The guard recognized us from previous visits and we were soon in front of Baoji who asked in alarm, 'What happened? Is Ma alright?'

'Yes, Baoji,' I replied. 'Bhai has got a job!'

'What! Where?'

'Imperial Bank! Here is the appointment letter.'

Bhai stood grinning from ear to ear while Baoji read the brief letter a few times before hugging him tightly. 'Well done, son. You have made me very proud!'

The news spread like wildfire and everybody came to

congratulate Baoji, Bhai and me. After some time, Baoji asked us to leave, promising to return home early. As we left, he gave some money to Bhai. 'Buy sweets, we will celebrate today.'

The news of Bhai getting a job—not just any job, but one at the prestigious Imperial Bank—was publicly celebrated. When yet another neighbour congratulated him, Baoji happily replied, 'I always knew Madan would do well, it was only a matter of time. When Rohan too returns from Australia, I will live the life of a rich man. A man with two wonderful sons need not work.' And he and Ma laughed merrily into the night.

Bhai's job had cross-city ramifications, providing considerable relief in Sangrur. Baoji and Ma immediately credited Hema with bringing good luck and believed that if not for her Bhai would have remained unemployed his entire life!

Bhai was thrilled beyond words and he confessed it was especially because his marriage was no longer at risk. I simply felt relieved that the sadness of my departure was mitigated.

Bhai got ready to work at the Imperial Bank in a new pair of trousers, shirt and tie and Baoji paid him the ultimate compliment: 'You look like an Englishman.' Ma, unfortunately, spoiled the show by putting a dark vermilion mark for luck on his forehead.

That evening, Bhai returned looking tired but happy. Ma immediately rushed to him with a glass of water and Baoji called him to sit by his side. Baoji asked, 'Madan, how was work today?'

After telling us about his first day, Bhai handed Baoji a gold embossed identity card and a bank account book with a broad smile. Bhai was now amongst a handful of Indians to hold an account in the esteemed bank. For many days thereafter, Baoji proudly showed the blank account book to all visitors.

Bhai had begun work in the middle of the month and it was soon pay day. That evening he went straight to Baoji and Ma, touched their feet and handed over his first salary to Ma. It was the fruition of a mother's dream and she wept tears of joy even as she and Baoji proudly hugged him.

The excitement of Bhai's new job ebbed and once again my imminent departure hung heavy upon us. A letter from Master Prasad asking Baoji to finalize the wedding date punctuated the routine. Baoji and Ma were already keen that Bhai get married before I left and so Pandit Hari Ram Shankar was immediately summoned. Bhai and I retreated to our room and we concentrated on eavesdropping.

Pandit Hari Ram Shankar, after carefully analyzing the horoscopes of Bhai and his bride, opened his panchangam and announced the most auspicious date fell three days before my departure. It was final: the marriage would take place after exactly twenty-seven days, on August 14.

Baoji handed Pandit Hari Ram Shankar some sweets and entrusted him with the task of immediately visiting Sangrur to seek concurrence from Master Prasad. He returned the next day to confirm their agreement and hand over boxes of sweets and gifts for the family.

With the date being fixed, Bhai looked relaxed while a sense of urgency enveloped Baoji and Ma; there was so much to be done!

Wedding cards were hurriedly printed and Baoji and Ma personally distributed them to friends and relatives.

Arrangements were made for our guests to stay and Baoji hired a halwai who pitched his tent outside our house to cook breakfast, lunch, dinner, and maintain constant supply of hot tea. Our house too was decorated with festoons and colorful lanterns.

On our last day together, before guests moved in and took over our house and neighbourhood, we reviewed my baggage and documentation. A lump formed in my throat when Bhai finally closed the clasp on my bag. He, Baoji and Ma were emotionally no better. When I remember those days, it seems unreal how we experienced two conflicting emotions at the same time: the joy of Bhai's wedding and the sorrow of my departure.

Guests began trickling in a few days before the wedding and it was as if a small town of relatives and friends had sprung up. There were numerous ceremonies and each evening womenfolk gathered to sing and dance. I would have enjoyed, but the prospect of my looming departure now filled me with dread.

Master Prasad and others welcomed us at the bus stop from where we took tongas to a community center where we had lunch and rested for a few hours.

As dusk fell, a band of musicians appeared, playing popular western music, creating a ripple of excitement as everyone quickly got ready—women in fine sarees and jewellery and men in kurta pajamas topped with red turbans. I wore a new suit and Bhai looked handsome in a fancy kurta pajama and turban with a curtain of gold threads falling in front of his eyes—the conventional gear of a bridegroom. After a brief ceremony Ma put a large red tilak on his forehead and he was ready.

As per tradition, Bhai had to go to his bride on horseback, but never having sat on one he was edgy and it didn't help that the horse was rather skittish and its handler, who tried to hold him still, old and frail. A few unsuccessful attempts later, Bhai was precariously placed on the saddle that he held on for dear life.

Our small group of torchbearers, musicians, friends and relatives brought life to the dark streets of Sangrur. After walking about a kilometer, we entered the now canopy covered alley where Master Prasad, looking striking in a pink turban, and others garlanded us and showered us with marigold petals.

The ceremony began and Bhai and the bride exchanged garlands before sitting around the holy fire. I concentrated on the available foodstuff till Baoji beckoned me to sit beside him.

Pandit Hari Ram Shankar sat as an observer while a pandit from the bride's side performed the rituals. The bride, wearing a heavily adorned saree with her face veiled completely, was escorted by her sisters and seated next to Bhai. The pandit renewed his incantations, vigorously feeding the holy fire with ghee. Bhai's shawl was tied to one end of Hema's saree and both circumambulated the holy fire seven times as the pandit poured in more ghee and chanted shlokas. They were declared 'Husband and Wife,' and all assembled showered them with flower petals.

It was exactly 3 a.m., that unearthly hour that is also the most auspicious. The bride was whisked away inside her house and while others lay wherever they could to get few winks, Baoji, Ma, Bhai and I were taken to the familiar living room. Baoji and Ma dozed off in no time and Bhai whispered to me. 'I wish I knew who was correct, you or I?'

'What do you mean?' I whispered back.

'I mean, I still don't know who my bride is. Did you get a look at your Bhabi?'

'No, but I am sure you'll find out soon.'

Bhai and I laughed uncontrollably, stifling the sounds as we were next to Baoji and Ma. Moreover, we realized people would look askance at Bhai laughing hysterically soon after his wedding.

We left Sangrur after an early breakfast. As we sat on tongas to go to the bus stop, Master and Mrs Prasad stepped forward with folded hands and tearfully asked Baoji and Ma to take care of their daughter.

Ours was a somber group that journeyed back home with everyone trying to comfort Bhai's bride, who cried her heart out for a long time. However, the mood changed dramatically the moment we reached Ambala. My Bhabi, Hema, entered her new home to the accompaniment of drums and merry music and it felt she had brought joy and happiness with her.

After the ceremonies over the next few days, our guests departed with customary sweets and gifts. Bhai and Bhabi occupied my bedroom and I shifted to the living room. Bhai finally looked at peace and Bhabi was already everyone's favorite.

On my last evening at home, Baoji brought samosas and jalebis, but I was too affected to eat; later in Sydney I would often salivate remembering these snacks. Relatives and neighbours kept dropping in with wide-eyed children unable to comprehend I was journeying abroad. There were also critics who announced that to travel across the sea was to lose one's religion and suffer its consequences. Each had a story which they insensitively recounted between munching tasty snacks served by Ma. If they were to be believed, their distant relative's distant relative had made a similar mistake never to return, either meeting a watery end or settling abroad with a foreign wife while back home their aged parents pined away to death. Despite misgivings and insinuated criticism of Baoji and Ma in allowing this foolish venture, they blessed me and wished me success. Studiously ignoring their scary prophesies, Ma made everyone comfortable; I knew her heart was breaking, but she played the perfect host.

Around 9 p.m. Baoji suddenly called it a day, which meant everyone had to leave; I guess the tension was building up in him. Finally, the house fell silent with only the four of us in the living room, Bhabi having retired early.

'Son,' said Baoji. 'I hope everything is packed carefully.'

'Yes Baoji, Bhai helped me. I have my passport, train ticket to Calcutta and ship ticket from there to Sydney.'

'What about money?'

'The five pounds you gave me shall be sufficient.'

'I know, but keep this too.' Baoji gave me a small folded envelope.

'No, Baoji, I don't need more money,' I protested mildly, but took the envelope. Inside lay assorted currency notes totaling eight pounds.

'Keep it safely,' Baoji gruffly ordered and I kept it in my passport; nobody argued with Baoji. Years later I learned Baoji had pawned Ma's jewellery.

Ma suddenly started crying softly and Bhai consoled her. 'Ma, he will be back soon.'

We sat emotionally choked; there was really nothing to be said. Thankfully Baoji got up and announced. 'Well, we leave at 4 a.m. so try to get some sleep.' Then, turning to Bhai he asked, 'Has Shankar been told? I hope the drunkard doesn't oversleep and make us miss the train.'

Bhai's friend, Shankar, plied a tonga and had offered to take us to the station.

'Don't worry, Baoji,' Bhai replied. 'He will be here on time.'

Baoji and Ma retired, though I knew they would get little sleep. Bhai and I were now alone in the living room and he asked one more time. 'So, all ready?'

'Of course, Bhai,' I replied with difficulty, struggling not to cry.

Bhai suddenly got up and said, 'Here, keep this too.' He had been holding something, which he now awkwardly thrust at me. It was a black and white photograph of us four, taken last Diwali.

'Thanks,' I muttered weakly with a heavy heart. Bhai appeared in no better shape. He briefly touched my shoulder and left.

I miserably settled on the couch looking at the photograph, and, pressing my face deep into the pillow so no one would hear, sobbed my heart out.

After some time, I heard footsteps and pretended to be asleep. It was Baoji. He came by my side, adjusted my quilt around me, and softly touched my cheek. I could feel his eyes boring into my face for a long time before he sighed and left, as silently as he had entered. I opened my eyes to see it was almost midnight...another four hours to go.

My sleep was troubled. I dreamed my kite was flying the highest of all, way above the clouds and climbing higher when its string broke, swiftly slipping from my palm, leaving me grasping at nothing even as I pleaded with Bhai, 'Stop it!' But my beautiful kite was already being tossed about by the winds and becoming ever smaller till I could see it no more. I rushed to Bhai, helplessly crying, 'Why didn't you stop it?' The very next moment I was being shaken awake. I opened my eyes and groggily saw Bhai by my side. It was time to leave.

I quickly took a bath and put on my newly-stitched shirt and trouser. Baoji, Ma, Bhai and Bhabi were already assembled in the living room and my suitcase was near the door.

We silently drank the hot tea that Ma had made for us when she asked me to stand. Wiping tears with her pallu, she performed a small puja, putting a tilak on my forehead and feeding me sweetened curd for good luck on the long journey. I touched her feet, then Baoji's, and finally Bhai and Bhabi's for their blessings. Ma hugged me tight, weeping uncontrollably. Baoji and Bhai tried to console her, but could not stop themselves from crying either. I tore away from her and went inside, pretending to look for something.

I first went to my old bedroom which already looked different but still felt like my own and I softly ran my hand across the walls and the bed as all my childhood memories came flooding back. Next, I went to Baoji and Ma's room to look one last time at everything familiar. My last stop was Ma's kitchen temple where, with no one watching, I closed my eyes and with folded hands prayed for a long, happy and healthy life for Baoji, Ma and Bhai. Knowing this would give them the greatest happiness, I also prayed for my own safe journey and quick return.

We stepped out into the dark silent night to find Shankar on his tonga, a shawl wrapped around him to keep away the slight chill. Bhai placed my suitcase under the seat and we all climbed on; Bhabi stayed back since it was considered inauspicious for a new bride to leave her husband's house the first time unless escorted by her brother.

Shankar nudged the sleepy horse with his foot and it sputtered to life, slowly picking speed. As we were about to leave the neighbourhood, I looked back one last time through teary eyes, and said a silent goodbye to my childhood.

It was a quiet journey except for the rhythmic beat of the horse's hooves. Shankar tried to make small talk, but then sensing the sober mood became quiet. We made good speed through deserted roads, reaching the station in about twenty minutes. Shankar knew exactly where to stop, expertly brushing away coolies pleading to be hired to carry my bag.

We got down bewildered; this was my first visit here and I didn't remember even Baoji or Bhai having come here before. Shankar confirmed from a passing coolie that the train was departing on time and said, 'You go on, I'll wait here.'

The platform was a beehive of activity with light smoky air enveloping people rushing to and fro and vendors loudly hawking trinkets and snacks, and tea sellers especially doing good business. Feeling out of sorts, we watched Bhai rapidly walk ahead with my suitcase to ascertain my berth number from a hand-written chart nailed to a notice board. He then signaled us and we walked urgently towards him as he entered a carriage.

The carriage was overcrowded and we made our way inside with difficulty. Bhai located my berth, the uppermost one, in one of the many cubicles. Each cubicle had six wooden berths, three on either side. An elderly couple sat on one of the bottom berths and Bhai put my suitcase under the other.

Bhai and I remained standing while Baoji and Ma greeted the elderly couple and sat down beside them. They got talking in no time and I learned the couple were a Mr and Mrs Ganguly from Calcutta who were returning from a wedding with their son and daughter-in-law. They were shocked to learn I was traveling alone, but then quickly assured my parents they would take care of me.

The train's whistle blew loudly and the noise increased manifold as visitors seeing off friends and relatives began exiting the carriage. Baoji and Ma too got up quickly and Bhai hugged me briefly and turned to leave; no one knew quite what to say and I silently followed them.

Baoji embraced me tightly at the door. 'Take care and write immediately on reaching.' There were tears in his eyes and I too was completely choked and only nodded in reply. Then, as Ma and Bhai hugged and kissed me goodbye we all began crying even as amused bystanders looked on. After another loud whistle, Baoji, Ma and Bhai hurriedly got down unto the platform, while I stood at the open door, looking at them through my tears. A sudden rush of late arrivals pushed me inside as I desperately rushed back to the open door.

Baoji, Ma and Bhai anxiously walked alongside the slowly moving train, trying to stay with me just that little bit longer. I waved and watched with blurry eyes the three people I loved the most walking faster, almost running, crying unashamedly and doing their best to keep me in sight. But we picked up speed and they were left behind—three forlorn figures helplessly watching me being taken away from them. At that moment, brushing my tears away, I looked hard at them, desperate to permanently capture their faces. Just then someone pushed me aside and when I looked again, even though I leaned out, I could no longer see them. I was on my own.

After some time, becoming conscious of fellow travelers, I entered the washroom and in its narrow confines, sheltered from prying eyes, with the noise of the train overpowering all sounds and my heart torn with grief, I cried my heart out. I don't know how long I was there but a banging on the door jolted me back to reality and I stepped out after quickly washing my face. I made my way to my cubicle where Mr Ganguly's son made space for me to sit, but saying I was sleepy I climbed unto my berth. My thoughts were with Baoji, Ma and Bhai and I wept silently till finally overcome by sleep.

It was early afternoon when I climbed down to join the Gangulys as we sped on our long journey passing farmlands and villages. Mr Ganguly, a retired professor of chemistry began discussing my future plans while Mrs Ganguly served hot food from tiffin boxes, not taking no for an answer. So I ate what was offered along with the food Ma had packed.

The train stopped often to refill coal and water, allowing us to stretch our legs and refill water bottles from hand pumps on the platform. This provided much-needed respite from the stuffy heat inside the compartment, but I took care to always stay near the door, lest the train suddenly pull away leaving me stranded in an unknown place.

Night fell and after dinner I lay on my berth watching a small fan turn slowly above me, making considerable noise and providing little relief. As we sped deeper into the night, I lay awake, shaking with each jerky movement of the train, imagining cities and villages we crossed and the lives of its people. Each moment I was moving further away from home, feeling miserable and dearly wishing it were not so.

Sleeping intermittently, I saw the train halt at dimly lit stations where new arrivals would try to locate their berths in the dark, banging their belongings here and there. But eventually order would be restored and after a mournful whistle we would move again, slowly picking up speed.

After what seemed like an eternity, darkness gave way to

early morning light and I got up, disheveled and somewhat disoriented. Almost miraculously, the night gone by had changed the traveling populace, with many awakening to find strangers in place of those with whom they had shared their lives the previous day. But this was expected and soon everybody was chatting and sharing eatables like old friends. It struck me then—this was my first ever night outside home.

Calcutta, Bengal: 1918

Lack of basics, such as a clean bath, coupled with stifling heat took its toll. I lay in a stupor, miserably looking out the dirty window as the train belched thick black smoke.

Finally, to everyone's palpable relief, after a full five days our train slowly chugged into the city of Calcutta. Everyone immediately got busy gathering their baggage while children excitedly strained at the windows to look out; not having much to repack I was ready in no time. Even as our train entered the station, scores of coolies engulfed it, agitatedly competing for customers. The moment it halted, everyone rushed to alight but Mr Ganguly asked me to wait and gave me directions to the port. We finally got down and, thanking the Gangulys for their kindness, I said goodbye.

Firmly holding my suitcase, I gingerly stepped out into the bright sunlight only to be instantly overpowered by the hustle and bustle. Disorientated by utter chaos, I tried to hail a rickshaw. When one finally claimed me after outshouting his rivals in native Bengali, I told him my destination and he set off, running rapidly through the congested streets towards the distant port across the Howrah Bridge. It tugged my heart to see a human reduced to a beast of burden, but I was soon transfixed by the teeming city of millions where the East India Company had set up its first trading post and which later became the capital of British India.

After around fifteen minutes, my rickshaw puller stopped at the port entrance, heavily perspiring, and demanded a fare of 10 paisa. Though Mr Ganguly had instructed to not give more than five, I didn't have the heart to bargain and he left happy, desperately seeking another customer. Suitcase in hand, I entered through the massive gate to find the port bristling with activity with men carrying jute gunnies on their backs into steamers. As I stood watching, a guard shouted from behind. 'Don't stand like a statue. Go register at the dormitory.'

The dormitory, a huge metal shed bearing a signboard 'P&O Shipping', was a few hundred feet away. Upon entering, a man inspected my travel papers and ticket and gave me a slip of paper with the number '10' on it, the number of my bed for the night. I also learned that my ship, chiefly a cargo vessel with limited space for around fifty passengers, would leave at first light.

In an adjoining hall were numerous wooden cots. After keeping my suitcase under the one bearing a metal plate engraved with the number '10', I lay down not quite knowing what to do next. Slowly more people walked in and by evening the hall was filled with fellow passengers, mostly soldiers and a few families. I bought tea from a small canteen at one end of the hall and carried the small earthen cup outside.

As I sat alone on a bench, sipping hot tea and eating food Mrs Ganguly had given me, I watched the moon and stars, wondering if they looked the same in Australia.

After some time, I walked to the pier and looked across the moonlit mass of water moving heavily and lapping anchored ships. It stretched indefinitely, far beyond what I could see, raising frightening visions of the dangers that lay ahead this ship. I shuddered, imagining it floundering in a furious storm and Baoji, Ma and Bhai receiving the tragic news of my end in the dark waters. The very next moment, I visualized my ship safely entering Sydney harbor with the entire city gathering to welcome me. Acutely conscious about my last night on my land, I spent as long as I could at the water's edge, feeling both dread and excitement.

I had hardly shut my eyes when amidst shrill whistles, a rough hand shook me awake. 'Come on, it is time to leave.' I got up with a start. It was still dark and nippy. 'Hurry up! The ship is sailing!' Urgent shouts surrounded me as everybody frantically got organized to board the ship—the *SS Intrepid*—so huge and solid that all my fears vanished. All of a sudden the darkness dissipated and the port came to life as screeching birds searched for food and men swarmed over ships carrying gunnies and baggage.

Our motley group stopped next to two men and an official who sat at a table near our ship. We lined up and one by one each person presented their papers that the official examined carefully before making few entries in a register. He then returned the papers, took out a token from a small box and handed it to the passenger who now had to climb a steep ladder and board the ship.

My turn soon came and I handed over my travel papers, which were scrutinized and duly registered before being returned along with a token numbered '5C'. Holding my suitcase with one hand and a guide rope with the other, I took a deep breath and stepped on the slightly swinging ladder. I climbed slowly, taking utmost care to maintain balance and not look down lest I feel giddy, and made the precarious climb without mishap. Panting for breath I found myself on deck, a wooden expanse stacked with barrels and machinery items. In front of me stood a giant of a man who asked for my token, which I handed over. I involuntarily looked over the side only to instantly jump back nervously.

Ignoring my reaction, the giant instructed me to follow him through a small door and began descending a narrow metal ladder. Carefully protecting my head from the low ceiling, I climbed down lower and lower behind him. It was tough and I was struggling till he finally looked back and said gruffly, 'Hand it over,' and took my suitcase. 'Don't want you to slip and break a leg. More trouble for me.'

Holding my suitcase, he expertly led me down till we stopped in a dark hallway. Despite the bright day outside little light entered here through the few mud-caked portholes. There was a deep rumbling and it seemed we had descended into the ship's bowels. Finally passing through few narrow doors, we entered a large gloomy hall where he stopped in front of a bed and declared grandly, 'Here you are, 5C. Your food will be brought here. Make sure you don't wander to the deck,' He deposited my suitcase on the floor and left.

I sat down to catch my breath and once my eyes adjusted to the dim light, I saw numerous metal bunks besides mine, much like in the port dormitory. This was obviously the ship's steerage housing the third-class compartment. It was a far cry from the sunswept deck I had imagined. Just when the depressing confinement was threatening to overpower, I saw a few people exit the hall from its far end and decided to follow.

My heart leaped with joy as I came out of the hall and into a spacious area with huge open windows from where cool air streamed in strongly. I hungrily gulped the fresh air, feasting my eyes on the wide, calm expanse of water and felt my anxiety disappear. I asked an old British gentleman sitting on a nearby bench, 'Good morning, Sir. Are we allowed here?'

'Yes, of course, son. You can be here anytime except at night as it can get rather nasty when the wind picks up and one may get washed overboard. Come, sit next to me and I will let you in on a secret.'

'Yes, Sir. Thank you,' I replied, feeling wonderful to converse with somebody.

'Well, I travel often and my secret is to always sleep here at night for it gets unbearably hot and humid inside. And I am not alone, but nobody says anything as long as it is done quietly. So, if you want to escape the uncomfortable quarters, come quietly once the supervisor leaves after dinner.'

'Yes, Sir.'

This gentleman, Mr Fraser, was a missionary from Sydney and was currently working in rural Bengal. He regaled me with stories of his adventures. He was traveling with his nephew who was exploring the ship at that time.

The ship's horn sounded loudly and the engine's noise increased manifold. I felt the ship shake free of its bondage and realized with a start we were leaving! Everyone excitedly crowded the open windows and I too rushed to them, squeezing past some men to look out. As the ship slowly pulled away, a small crowd at the pier waved goodbye to friends and relatives. Straining my neck, I looked at the open deck above on which stood the ship's officers and beautifully dressed men and women, obviously first-class passengers, happily waving back. The moment was infectious and I too began waving to no one in particular. With a final loud blowing of the horns, we left the harbour.

The fascinating spectacle of the ship's movement across the ocean had me rooted, tightly clenching the railing, my heart thumping excitedly. With cool wind blowing and random droplets caressing my face, I gazed for long at the slowly disappearing city and the all-enveloping deep waters, now a shimmering golden sheet under the rising sun. The world suddenly appeared too vast and I longed for the comfort of my family.

We slowly rolled onwards till the shore was an imagined speck on the horizon. Each time I thought we had stopped, I rushed to the side only to realize that the ship continued to steadily move deeper into the seemingly unending ocean. The early morning breeze warmed and soon heat and humidity began to affect everyone except a few children playing tag and some soldiers who were obviously inebriated though it was not yet past noon. Feeling sleepy, I returned to my bed for a short nap and found a cup of tea and thick buttered bread placed by its side. Looking out of the dirty porthole, I had breakfast, dipping bread into the cold tea to make it soft and chewable.

Feeling refreshed, I headed back to find Mr Fraser who was talking to a young man. He was about my age and as I hesitated, Mr Fraser beckoned, 'Come, come. I was wondering where you were. This is my nephew, Mike.'

Mike had a contagious smile and with Mr Fraser looking on benignly, we were soon chatting comfortably. He was exactly my age and on his first visit to India—a holiday promised by his uncle. He was impressed on finding out that I was going to the Academy of Sciences and confessed that he found studies 'too bloody tooof'. Mike suddenly asked, 'Why, you must be a prince! How come you are traveling steerage? Lost your kingdom, have you?'

'Come on, Mike,' I smiled. 'Stop joking. You surely saw in Calcutta that not every Indian is a king or prince.' I was to learn later that most foreigners knew India only as a land of fabulously rich kings and queens living in luxurious palaces going on tiger hunts atop elephants bedecked with jewels.

Time passed easily, but soon after I enjoyed the magnificent spectacle of a sunset at sea, daylight began fading and my fears returned. By late evening the day's tranquility was dramatically transformed and the placid waters turned into a fearsome monster. Huge waves noisily crashed incessantly against the ship, which felt like it could disintegrate any moment. The open hall, a pleasant refuge all day, now appeared treacherous as wave after wave crashed in from one side and out of the other, threatening to cast the struggling vessel and those on it into the depths of the furious ocean. Of course, at the first sign of the terrible storm we all had rushed to the relatively secure steerage. But here too there was little respite and the heart-wrenching cries of women and children resounded in its confines.

I lay cowering on my bed, desperately praying to as many Gods as I could remember. Soon, people began getting sick, helplessly throwing up and the pungent smell of vomit hung heavy, making me feel queasy. I tried to go to the bathroom, but the ship was rolling heavily and my legs refused to respond, sending a wave of panic through me. I could not control any longer. Just then someone thrust a paper bag at me and I threw up in it. I retched repeatedly, finally lying back exhausted, unable to think or act. I had no idea when, despite the mayhem, I fell asleep.

I woke up around noon, weak and dehydrated. Mr Fraser was by my side to cheerfully welcome me back to life. 'So, mate, you looked a fright. If I hadn't handed you the bag on time you would have made a fine mess.'

I looked around sheepishly and saw the hall was reasonably clean; deck hands had obviously washed away all traces of disorder. Mr Fraser handed me a cup of tea and commanded, 'Drink this. You lost a lot of fluids. The good thing is it won't happen again, everyone gets seasick only once.'

It took some time, but after having tea and a few biscuits and washing myself clean, I felt much better. Indeed, Mr Fraser was quite correct and I did not get seasick again. It also helped that we were back in calmer waters.

After fourteen days we docked at Rangoon when, to everyone's amusement, I mistakenly thought we had reached Sydney. Sea weary and longing to stretch my legs on the welcoming landmass I readied to leave the ship, but was informed that third-class passengers were not extended this luxury. Finally, after a three-day halt during which we practically boiled in heat, we sailed onwards. We stopped once more, at Jakarta, but this time I did not torture myself with the thought of getting down on land.

We were one big family in the steerage, bonded together by shared difficulties and fear of nightly storms. I still spent most of my time with Mr Fraser and Mike but felt equally comfortable with others; the soldiers were an especially merry lot, playing cards and drinking all day. Ship hands served snacks and meals at fixed hours that we ate in the open hall, especially enjoying dinner under a silvery moon that lit the dark waters as stars twinkled above.

One morning, Mr Fraser suddenly pointed far out to sea and loudly announced, 'Sydney!'. The news spread like wildfire and we all crowded the sides excitedly, peering intently at the distant shoreline. I could scarcely believe my journey was over and my exhilaration knew no bounds, but there was also a twinge of sadness since a vast ocean now separated me from my family.

Sydney, New South Wales: 1918–1923

Mid-afternoon, the *SS Intrepid* majestically steamed into Port Jackson to the accompaniment of bells ringing from two berthed vessels; my journey had taken exactly sixty-nine days. There was a festive air onboard and I was ready with my suitcase repacked neatly as I excitedly watched the approaching shoreline alongside Mr Fraser and Mike. Finally, after considerable effort, the crew secured ropes unto bollards and our ship slid against the side with a loud thump as metal struck wood. The instant it happened, a loud cheer went up and everyone began waving to people on the pier. I impatiently looked forward to my first steps on foreign soil.

Deck hands brought a narrow, wooden walkway and after securing it, opened a small access gate. We were instructed beforehand to wait our turn and patiently watched first-class passengers disembark and leave the pier.

After almost an hour of waiting, I eagerly stepped on the walkway, no longer afraid to look down from a height. With a deep breath I confidently stepped on land, my excitement instantly transforming to mortal fear as my legs trembled and I felt faint. Luckily, Mr Fraser held me and, looking at the worry on my face, assured me, 'Don't worry, son. This is usual after a long sea journey. It will take time to get used to be walking on land again, but you'll be alright.'

It had been frightening, but sure enough after some

time I managed to walk, gingerly at first and then normally; having unconsciously adapted to the uneven sway of the ship I needed to readjust to firm land! I joined the queue along with Mr Fraser and Mike, and when my turn came, presented my papers to the uniformed officers. 'So, you are a student,' the officer commented after seeing the Academy's admission papers. Then, giving me a stamped paper—my official entry permit into the city of Sydney—he added, 'Welcome to Australia, mate. Stay out of trouble.'

Mr Fraser and Mike gave me directions to the Academy and we parted at the port gate. Hoisting my suitcase, I began walking tentatively onwards when suddenly wonderstruck I stood still. Everything was so different, so foreign! The people, buildings, roads, everything! Even the breeze felt and smelt different—cool, refreshing and enticing. I don't know how long I stood motionless till I was jolted out of my reverie by a friendly tap on my shoulder. 'Mate, you lost?' It was Mike! As we walked on, he explained. 'The way you were walking, I was afraid you would bang into a tram, so I thought I better keep my eye on you some more time.'

With Mike by my side, I was soon enjoying the sights of Sydney, a city dramatically different from Ambala and Calcutta. Thrilled beyond words and tiredness now all but forgotten, I merrily walked through market places and parks till Mike left me in front of an imposing sandstone building, promising to look me up later. I was at the Academy of Sciences, my home for the next few years.

Diffidently entering the courtyard, I followed the signage to a stern bespectacled lady at a reception desk. Taking a deep, calming breath, I stepped up to present my admission papers, instantly feeling at ease when she smiled warmly. After checking my name against a list, she said pleasantly, 'Welcome to the Academy, Mr Rohan. I hope you had a good journey. Mr Hughes will guide you to your dorm.'

Mr Hughes was a tall man perhaps in his sixties with a shock of silvery white hair. He appeared to be sorting mail a few feet away and came over upon hearing his name. 'Welcome, mate. Let me help you with your bag.'

I silently followed Mr Hughes down a large hallway with beautiful paintings every few feet. He was a friendly soul and as we walked, he explained he was the Academy's oldest employee and doubled up as janitor, cook, and handyman. Then he asked, 'And you are Prince Rohan, right?'

'Yes, Sir,' I instinctively replied, realizing my mistake as soon as the words escaped my mouth but before I could correct myself Hughes continued, 'I must visit India to hunt tigers! Last year, we had the Prince of Mauraj who had a wonderful collection of guns and so much baggage it wouldn't fit into the dorm! I hope you don't have the same problem when your bags reach. By the way, are you related to His Highness? I hear royal families are related.'

'No, Sir,' I replied quietly, my mind reeling. We were now before a closed door that Hughes opened to grandly announce to nobody in particular. 'Gentlemen, please welcome Prince Rohan from India, your new dorm mate.'

I was in a long rectangular hall with around ten boys, some sitting on beds and others at study tables. All of them paused their respective activities to look at me. Hughes led me to a bed at one end and placing my suitcase by its side, said, 'Here you are, Highness. I am sure you will settle down soon. Do let me know if I can be of any service.'

'Thank you, Sir,' I replied. Watching Hughes's receding back I suddenly felt alone, not knowing what to do next. Then a tall, gangly boy lying on the adjoining bed got up and held out his hand. 'I am Mark. Welcome, Prince Rohan.'

'Hello, Mark. Please call me Rohan,' I replied, as he shook my hand warmly.

Within the next few minutes Mark introduced me to the other boys, who approached with a diffidence and curiosity I had not experienced before. Most had never met anybody from India before and were fascinated to meet a 'real blue-blooded prince', as Josh, a freckled, red-headed boy with an easy smile put it. By the time the bell rang for tea I had answered umpteen questions about my fictional palaces and with everyone going out of the way to make me comfortable, my uncertainties vanished.

That night, after a hearty dinner in the mess, I lay on my bed looking out of the window. The moon looked the same, as at home, yet it felt different. I missed Baoji, Ma and Bhai but I could hardly contain my excitement and Professor Hardayal's words that I had embarked on the most enriching experience of my life rang in my ears. There was only the small matter of being mistaken as royalty and after deliberation I sat down to fix it.

Respected Baoji, Ma, and Bhai,

Namaste. I hope you are all well. It seems like I have been away from home for years. This place is very far, so far that it will be another month or more when you get this letter.

I really enjoyed the journey here. On the train, it was remarkable to be passing through towns I had only read or heard about. Thanks to the Ganguly family I did not feel alone, but it was a very long journey and I was glad when it got over.

Calcutta fascinated me. It must surely be the biggest city in the world with millions of people and huge, majestic buildings; I am sure entire Ambala will fit inside the railway station itself! I reached the port without difficulty and slept in a dormitory there.

Seeing the ocean for the first time was frightening. It stretches for miles and the huge mass of water moves as if a gigantic animal is tossing and turning. I was initially apprehensive that my ship could actually cross the ocean, but felt comfortable after meeting some regular travelers. We stopped at Rangoon and Jakarta, but were not allowed to get down; these places are also under British rule. Each day I wished you all were with me to enjoy the unbelievably beautiful sights.

It took sixty-nine days to reach here. Sydney is a beautiful town: clean, nice and markedly different from back home. Interestingly, I first thought people here speak a foreign language before realizing it is English, but accented, quite different from that of the British officers at Ambala.

I am told my Academy is the best in Australia. There are twenty boys in my dorm and I have already made a few friends. The food tastes different but I will get used to it. It is, of course, nothing compared to Ma's tasty cooking!

Please tell Professor Hardayal I will soon meet his friend, Professor Hubertson, and convey his regards.

Lots of love,

Rohan

P.S: Bhai, when you write please address me as 'Prince Rohan'. I'll explain later.

The Academy was a wonderland: its dorms, gym, library, cafeteria, everything so neat and wonderful. For the first time ever I actually enjoyed sitting in a classroom! There were minor hiccups, such as understanding the accent, but as the only Indian student that year, the entire Academy seemed to have adopted me and I soon felt at home. It helped that Professor Hardayal's tuition enabled me to breeze through my placement tests and when fellow students began asking for assistance, it gave me tremendous confidence.

One day, there was conspicuous excitement as Principal Keating announced that Professor Hubertson was visiting to give a talk to the new students. This was evidently the high point of our initiation and Professor Keating detailed Professor Hubertson's achievements and advised us to listen to him carefully.

We assembled in the auditorium after lunch to await the arrival of the chief guest. I sat in the front row next to Mark, now a close friend. There was a sudden flurry of activity as a number of professors, all in formal black robes, entered along with the chief guest. 'He certainly looks distinguished,' Mark quipped. 'We are going to get frightfully bored. Mark my words: the more distinguished a speaker, the more boring he is.' I stifled a chuckle, trying to appear attentive.

Professor Keating introduced Professor Hubertson, inviting him to share his thoughts. A hush descended as Professor Hubertson made his way to the lectern. His was a welcome speech with a difference and, contrary to Mark's assertion, extremely entertaining. Extolling us to work hard, he insisted we enjoy life, regaling us with stories of his own student days. In closing, Professor Hubertson looked directly at me. 'I must confess I have a special interest in being here today. You see, as a student I was terrible in Chemistry and may even have dropped out but for Harry, my best friend, who encouraged me to not give up. Unfortunately, due to personal reasons he returned to his country and the world of science lost a genius. Thankfully today we have amongst us his student, Rohan, who my friend assures will set new standards of excellence.'

The entire hall burst out clapping as I sat astounded, not knowing how to react to this unexpected attention. Even as everyone looked at me, I desperately tried to remember who 'Harry' was before it struck me...Professor Hardayal!

Tea was on the lawns and as the professors gathered around Professor Hubertson, we students chatted in small groups a little distance away. Mark and others immediately labeled me a 'genius' and I became the target of few good-natured jokes. Just then, a senior approached to say Professor Hubertson wanted a word with me and the crowd parted as I was led to him.

'Well, Rohan,' said Professor Hubertson, after I wished him respectfully. 'We meet finally. Harry has told me so much of you in his letters. I hope you are comfortable.'

'Yes, Sir,' I replied diffidently, conscious the entire gathering was watching with interest the great professor interacting with a newcomer.

'How is our friend, Harry?'

'He is doing very well, Sir.'

'When you write to him, tell him I remember him very much. I admire how easily he sacrificed everything to go back to look after his mother. It was a loss to science and to me personally. But I am glad you are here now and I feel that through you I am closer to Harry.'

'Yes, Sir,' I replied not knowing quite what to say.

Just then Professor Keating approached us and Professor Hubertson declared, 'George, Rohan here is my special guest. From time to time I would like to know about his progress.' Laying an affectionate hand on my shoulder, he said, 'I will be in touch. I would like to know more about dear Harry once you settle down. And do let me know if you need anything here.'

'Absolutely, Sir,' I replied. 'Thank you very much.'

Professor Keating interjected, 'We will take good care of Rohan.'

I walked back to my friends who were all in obvious awe of me. I was, as Mark put it succinctly: 'A blue blooded prince and a personal friend of Australia's greatest scientist!'

My joy at this newfound importance was overshadowed as I suddenly remembered how we ingrates had underestimated Professor Hardayal back home. I had personally been ungracious despite all he did for me. I had not even written to him after reaching here! I felt ashamed and was determined to make amends.

Later that evening I penned a letter to Professor Hardayal. Knowing it would please him considerably, I recounted Professor Hubertson's exact words and the high esteem in which he was held and concluded by sincerely thanking him for everything he had done for me. As I closed the envelope, I felt sorry for not truly appreciating Professor Hardayal until pointed out by a complete stranger.

Mr Hughes continued to bestow me with special attention. I found this extremely disconcerting but kept up the charade. He often sympathized at the assumed delay of my baggage. I could not get myself to tell him that I wore the best Baoji could afford and even if I stayed a hundred years at the Academy no more bags would arrive. Finally, one day I told him that my baggage was lost at sea and I had directed my minister not to send any more clothes for I now preferred to live simply like the rest of the boys. Hughes unexpectedly disclosed this to everybody and one by one my new friends came up to share their best clothes, an offer I took up readily. As a result, I was often the best dressed when we went to the markets at Queen Victoria building or Kings Cross!

Studies were rigorous but after being recognized by Professor Hubertson the teachers were especially kind to me. Life soon fell into a routine—I woke up at 6 a.m. for exercises, followed by a quick bath and hearty breakfast, classes began at 8 a.m. in the academic building, a short walk from the dorm, and went on till lunch, afternoon classes began at 1 p.m., mostly lab work, and we were free by 4 p.m. Some boys would then play cricket and others football and after tea at about 5.30 p.m. we would invariably go to town, walking the streets and enjoying the sights. We had to return to the dorm by 7 p.m. and there were strict penalties for violating the deadline.

As time passed, my friends took me to their homes over weekends, though sometimes I had nowhere to go and would feel bad Ambala was so far. On such days I explored the city by myself so it wasn't too bad after all.

At times, I met up with Mike at a local store where he worked and we would then take in the sights of Sydney; he knew the city inside out and showed me places no tourist would see. I genuinely enjoyed his company though I knew Mark and others frowned upon our friendship and once someone commented obliquely that my father, the king, would have a fit if he heard I was hobnobbing with somebody like Mike! But they were good blokes and I didn't mind; Mike remained special since he was the first friend I made on my journey.

After about four months, I received my first letter from home. Just holding the brown envelope bearing my name in Bhai's familiar writing made me realize how much I missed Baoji, Ma and him. Before my emotions overcame me, I went to the garden to be alone and it was only after several minutes that I slowly opened the letter. It was written in Urdu and seeing the familiar script and visualizing Bhai writing with Baoji and Ma sitting beside him made me teary even before I read a single line.

My dear Rohan,

Baoji and Ma were enquiring about your letter from the postman every day and were overjoyed on finally hearing from you. We are happy you reached safely and have settled down. You are fortunate to be having amazing experiences and seeing places we otherwise only hear or read about.

Your letter caused considerable excitement. First, the postman announced to the entire neighbourhood that he had a 'foreign' letter then your friends kept asking me for its stamps. Baoji took it everywhere and read it to everyone and has now kept it prominently in the living room, readily available to be shown to guests.

Baoji and Ma are proud you are doing what nobody in the family has done before, but are also sad you are so far. Initially, Ma took it the worst...she would place a plate for you on the dining table and weep. Baoji doesn't say much, but he too misses you badly. Each day and event reminds them of your absence. The other day Ma said Diwali is approaching but she does not even like to think of it since you are not here. However, they are trying to adjust and I feel your Bhabi's presence is helping. When I got my salary Baoji joked that had you been home you would have taken it all! And last night I heard him assure Ma that it is good you are away; he was referring to the massacre by General Dyer at Jallianwala and the general unrest. Anyway, you need to focus on your studies and make them proud.

Your birthday is approaching, so here's wishing you a very happy birthday from all of us. I am keeping a £5 note in this letter for you to treat your friends. I know it's a risk but it will be expensive to send a money order, which will also take much longer. Anyway, write back immediately when you get it so I can relax.

Take good care and write regularly. Ma is saying you should eat well and Baoji wants me to remind you to follow his safety rules!

Lots of love,
Bhai

The letter was addressed to 'Prince Rohan' just as I had requested Bhai in my letter to him. Baoji had apparently lost his temper at my ludicrous suggestion, telling everybody in the vicinity that the fraud I suggested was a sure sign I would end up in jail. But he had penned the title.

That night, I read Bhai's letter over and over again, visualizing firecrackers bursting in the sky in far off Ambala and friends and relatives joyfully hugging each other while celebrating Diwali. I imagined Baoji, Ma and Bhai perfunctorily performing the traditional prayers and lighting lamps, thinking of me all the time. Longing to be home I wept silently into my pillow.

I might not have realized that I had been here for exactly one year had Bhai not mentioned this in his letter. This made me realize that the first year of parting is the toughest and having completed a cycle of missed birthdays and festivals, I had emerged stronger. I was popular with both classmates and teachers, and was elected president of the Poetry Club and editor of the Academy newsletter. Also, the first year's result had just been announced and I had topped. Of course, on hearing sporadic news of the struggle back home against the British, I would momentarily worry about Baoji, Ma and Bhai but it was not too disturbing.

Summer vacations were to begin shortly and I had received invitations to visit half a dozen friends, but I needed extra credits to graduate and return home earlier. Luckily, Professor Hubertson was looking for interns and selected me; he was now an integral part of my life, his summons when he visited the Academy initially created a flutter of excitement but the novelty wore off and I routinely met with him in the boardroom.

One day, Hughes mentioned that Professor Hubertson had visited the Academy and, surprised he had not asked for me, I rang his home at the spur of the moment, feeling relieved when he responded happily.

'Rohan! It is so good to hear from you. I wished to meet you today, but was told you were in lab so I did not disturb you.'

Without even asking why I had called, he invited me over the coming Saturday!

With suppressed excitement, I thought of nothing else the entire week. Principal Keating granted me permission and even appeared envious for it was rare to be invited to the great man's house. Finally, the long awaited day arrived and dressed in my best I took the bus to Professor Hubertson's house.

It was a one-hour ride and while enjoying the beautiful countryside, it struck me that I actually knew very little of Professor Hubertson personally, except that he had devoted his life to research and never married. I looked forward to my time with him and to later recount the experience to my friends.

After alighting, I asked a grocer to reconfirm the direction. 'Excuse me, Sir, could you please direct me to Cherrywood cottage?'

'My pleasure, young man. So, Professor Hubertson is having a visitor today!'

'Why, do you know the professor?'

'Mate, everybody knows the good professor. After all, he is the only celebrity we have.'

I was soon in front of a lovely country home with a small wooden gate opening to a cobbled driveway through a beautiful garden blooming with flowers and fruit trees. As I entered hesitantly, a loud cheerful voice greeted me. 'Rohan, welcome to my refuge!' It was Professor Hubertson, emerging from a potting shed in the garden.

'Hello, Professor. Thank you very much for having me. You have a lovely garden indeed.'

'I wish I could spend more time on it, but you know how it is. Come, let's go inside and I'll get you a cool drink.'

I thoroughly enjoyed the next few hours. In his own environs, Professor Hubertson revealed a side I could not have imagined—delighting me with humorous anecdotes of his youth and mimicking his colleagues, men of considerable stature in the scientific world. He was also a wonderful cook and I enjoyed the feast he had especially prepared for me. Then just as I was beginning to feel completely at home, it was time to leave.

'Well, Rohan. Thanks for coming. The hours just flew by and I had a fantastic time. You must visit again soon.'

'I too had a wonderful time and felt like I was home.'

'You must miss your family, no?'

'Yes, I do. The first few months were tough, but now studies keep me so busy I hardly get time to think of them. I look forward to the day I will graduate and go back.'

'I understand.'

'Professor, do you mind if I ask you a personal question?'

'What is it? Go ahead.'

Pointing to few photos on the mantelpiece I asked, 'I could not help but notice these photos of you with this girl. Who is she, Sir? I mean, I heard you stay alone.'

Professor Hubertson picked up a photo to show me. 'This is my niece, Jenny. She is all the family I have. She is about your age. Her parents—-my brother and his wife—-died in an accident when she was a child. She studies in Rosemary School and stays there since I travel a lot. However, she is here most weekends and I expect her today too, but rather late. I am sure you both will get along well when you meet her someday.'

My curiosity satiated, I thanked Professor Hubertson for the lovely day and took leave. Later at the Academy, I felt a strange thrill upon remembering the lovely girl in the photo.

Preoccupation with a girl was a novel experience and I had a poor opinion of guys who hung around them. Back home my interaction with the opposite sex was limited to cousins and neighbours, all categorized as 'sisters', the relationship being sanctified during Rakhi when brothers swore to protect their sisters. In any case, I lived in mortal fear of Baoji, who would have skinned me alive at the slightest hint of a scandal.

The first time I met Jenny, I didn't even know it was her.

Caught up in studies, my memory of her dimmed, leaving behind an unsure recollection. But one day, upon hearing Professor Hubertson was expected, my infatuation revived so strongly that before I knew it I was plotting to get an invite from him so I could meet Jenny.

Praying he would send for me, my eyes kept darting to the door, but the minutes slipped by and no messenger came. Finally losing patience, I left my classroom on the pretext of going to the bathroom, planning instead to walk by the boardroom so I could run into the professor.

I cautiously made my way downstairs. Being out of class without permission was viewed seriously, but I was confident that once I met the professor it would be presumed he had summoned me. Nearing the boardroom, I slowed my pace to a crawl, my nervousness increased with each passing second, but to my disappointment the door remained tightly shut. Almost giving up I turned away from the door.

Just then, the boardroom's door burst open and a girl rushed out. Before I could react, she ran straight into me, knocking me down and setting off loose papers flying everywhere.

Panic-stricken for being in the wrong place at the wrong time, I instantly rushed about collecting the papers as she got up, brushed herself and repeatedly apologized. 'I am so sorry. I should have watched out. I do hope you are not hurt.' I hurriedly handed over the papers, without so much as a proper glance at her and ran upstairs without replying.

Halfway up the stairs, I stopped to look back but she had left. The brief glimpse I had been able to capture—her beautiful face, light blue eyes, shining blonde hair, and glowing skin, captivated me like nothing else before.

I resumed work but was distracted, constantly thinking

of the most stunning beauty I had ever seen, feeling a strange sensation each time I relived our encounter. I was in love! With someone I did not even know!

I spent the day daydreaming about my newfound love. So infatuated was I that I kept missing the mark during our basketball game and Pat commented loudly. 'Rohan's mind is elsewhere. I think he has found a girl.'

Everybody laughed and the moment passed, but it was enough for John to corner me after the game. He was a good friend and I knew that once his curiosity was aroused he would not rest till he had successfully badgered the information out of me. Sure enough, as we sat for tea, he cajoled. 'Come on, Rohan, is it true?'

'What is true?'

'What Pat just said, that you have found a girl?'

'Don't be silly. How could I possibly meet any girl without you knowing?'

'But you *do* have a lost look about you since afternoon.'

'You are just imagining it.'

'Why don't you tell me the truth?'

'I just told you there is nothing to tell!'

This went on for some time with John refusing to give up. I ended up telling him all about the girl I had run into but not having actually met the girl I *really* had nothing much to tell. He was persistent and I finally promised to disclose my love story to him at night. I was merely negotiating peace, but as time passed I felt the need to share my feelings with someone, and who better than John? Why, maybe he could even help me find my mystery girl!

After dinner, John and I worked on a project due for

submission shortly. He had not brought up the topic again and I longed for him to say something so I could talk about her. Thankfully, he did not let me down and as soon as our work was done, he asked, 'Remember your promise?'

'What promise?' I feigned innocence.

'Don't josh, you promised you'll tell me about your girlfriend.'

Hearing him say, 'girlfriend', brought a warm glow all over me. 'OK. But swear to keep it to yourself.'

'I promise. You know I can keep a secret.'

I knew that was far from the truth, but I went ahead and recounted the day's incident.

'I have been unable to get her off my mind. When I saw the photograph of Professor Hubertson's niece, I thought I was in love with her, but the girl I bumped into today is strikingly more beautiful and is driving me crazy. But I don't even know her name, I really don't know what to do!'

He was clearly amused at how I could first fall in love with a girl in a photograph and then with a complete stranger but realizing I was serious, he replied after a thoughtful pause.

'Well, to find her we must first know what she was doing in the boardroom.'

'Yes, but how?'

'There is a way. One needs a visitor's pass to enter the Academy. So, Mr Steve at the gate must have her details.'

'Yes!' I shouted gleefully, annoying those trying to sleep. 'You are brilliant!'

'Thank you. I know I am,' John replied immodestly.

But then a thought struck me. 'How will we get the information from Mr Steve?'

'That's where your royal status comes in.'

'What do you mean?'

'Hughes will do anything his royal highness asks. Simply

ask him to ask Mr Steve, they are good friends. It should then be easy to find the girl as we don't get many visitors and you know the approximate time.'

'Yes, I could do that, but Hughes will tell everyone. Anyway, I don't think I will see her again so might as well forget it.'

'Don't be daft. How can you give up? Tell Hughes you need the list for a project.'

It seemed easy the way John explained it and when once again the image of the stunning girl flashed before my eyes, I readily agreed. After all, I had nothing to lose.

Next morning, Hughes agreed rather easily when I promised him a ride on my royal elephant when he visited India and sure enough, at tea he handed me the visitors list. I quickly took it and went to my dorm. John had seen the exchange and followed me.

The dorm was deserted and I excitedly sat on my bed going through the two sheets of badly scribbled names with times of entry and exit against them. With John peering over my shoulder I quickly scanned the names numerous times but found no mention of any girl. Deeply disappointed, I silently handed over the list to John, though he had already read it. After a few minutes of silent perusal he gave his solemn verdict: 'No girl entered the Academy yesterday.'

'How can that be? Surely I did not imagine her?'

'This only means she came in without a pass and you say she was carrying some documents that you helped her collect after she bumped into you. The conclusion is obvious.'

'What do you mean?'

'She was a thief who came for those papers and you helped her steal them!'

John was well known for his fertile imagination but this

was ludicrous and I immediately pounced on him. 'You have lost your senses! What is there to steal here? And can you imagine a theft by the most gorgeous girl in the world in the middle of the day when everyone, including Professor Hubertson, was in the boardroom? You are indeed a nut!'

John digested my words silently, looking pained at my sharp criticism. 'I concede a theft is difficult when a meeting is on, but I don't agree there is nothing to steal here or that beautiful girls can't be crooks.'

I tried to placate him for I still required him. I asked him politely. 'What do you think really happened, and who was that girl?'

'I don't know, but let me think.'

We both thought hard and long, but found no explanation. Finally, John left after promising to come up with something and I carefully tore the list, flushing it down the drain. However, all evening my mind was on the mystery girl.

That weekend, John and I deliberated and, to my disappointment, he told me he had given up. Realizing it was a hopeless situation I too grudgingly gave up my quest. Somehow at that very moment I again thought of Professor Hubertson's niece.

To my utter discomfiture, my fascination became the talk of the dorm, thanks to John, who despite his promise shared it with others. Day in and day out my friends baited me saying that they knew the girl. There was simply no escape and out of sheer desperation I decided to stay out of everyone's sight and rang Professor Hubertson. He immediately invited me even as I guiltily realized this had been my original plan before running into the girl.

Saturday morning dawned bright and sunny and I awoke with a surprising clarity, as one does after a fever breaks, knowing instantly I was past my fixation. It had been so out of character for me and I mentally gave the episode a quiet burial, realizing I had even lost interest in the professor's niece. Solemnly determined to shun even the thought of girls, I hurried off to Professor Hubertson after a quick brunch. On the bus journey all I thought was of having a relaxed time and discussing a few path-breaking researches.

I felt on top of the world as I hurried through the marketplace. Just as I was about to cross Dymocks, I retraced my steps and entered it. After perusing the large number of titles, with great deliberation I choose a thin book, *Complexities of Rare Elements* and got it gift wrapped; I was always careful with my limited funds, but this small token of appreciation was long overdue for all that the good professor had done for me.

The garden gate was open and as I entered, I became conscious of the gift and the protest it would attract; the professor was well aware of my background and finances. Deciding to gift the book when I was leaving, I slipped it under my shirt.

Professor Hubertson welcomed me warmly and I was soon enjoying a cup of fine Indian tea he had especially made for me. Our conversation was stimulating and I soon lost track of time. He seemed distracted and kept glancing out of the window, so I asked, 'Are you expecting someone?'

'Yes, my niece Jenny should have reached by now. Remember, I told you last time that she visits over weekends? If she doesn't come in soon I will have to go to the bus stop to inquire.'

Jenny! I had completely forgotten about her! Instantly conscious how my affection had shifted to the mystery girl and my latest tribulations, I got up. 'I think you should wait some more, Sir. Maybe she missed the bus and is on the next one, but if you'll please excuse me I will head back now. I have an exam coming up.'

'Hold it, son. What's the hurry? You just got here. Also, you must meet Jenny. I had mentioned to her that you would be here and she wanted to say hello.'

'If you don't mind Professor, I'll meet her next time.'

'She will be disappointed. I had told her so much about you and she really wanted to meet you.'

Just then Professor Hubertson's face lit up as he heard the garden gate open and looking out he smiled. 'Well, it's too late now. Here she comes.'

Professor Hubertson got up to open the door as I began to wish I were elsewhere. I caught a fleeting look at a petite, beautiful blonde who entered the room like a breath of fresh air and was immediately enveloped in a bear hug by Professor Hubertson. 'Thank God you are here! I was getting worried.'

I heard a muffled, 'Hi Uncle. It's really good to see you,' before Jenny wriggled out of the professor's arms, blushing upon seeing a witness to the emotional show. Smiling pleasantly, she approached me holding her hand out. 'Hi. It is so nice to meet you, Rohan. I have heard so much of you from Uncle.'

She was my mystery girl! Dumbfounded by the beautiful vision and unable to utter a single syllable, I simply gaped as she came closer. I was jolted out of my trance by Professor Hubertson who asked with mild amusement. 'Rohan, won't you say hello?'

Stuttering a barely audible 'hello' I briefly touched her

fingers in a handshake, embarrassing her all the more, but recovering quickly she asked me to sit before going upstairs to her room, carrying her case.

Professor Hubertson busied himself in the kitchen and I quickly picked a magazine and pretended to read. My mind was in a whirl and my heart beat rapidly even as things slowly began to make sense, though it was obvious she had no recollection of running into me the other day. There was no question of leaving now and, taking a deep breath to steady my nerves, I determined to make up for lost time, completely forgetting my resolve to stay away from girls.

'Jenny, lunch is ready,' Professor Hubertson called out and after a minute or so she bounced down the stairs looking utterly radiant.

'Rohan, you must tell me about India. I am so fascinated by its kings and elephants and tigers. By the way, I hope you did not have to wait long, I missed my bus and took the next one.'

She had assumed I was here for her! My earlier awkwardness forgotten quickly, we were soon chatting merrily, joined from time to time by Professor Hubertson, who set the table insisting he needed no help. She was a livewire with an opinion on everything and much as I was enjoying her company and drinking in her beauty, I realized I stood little chance.

After some time, she suddenly got up with a laugh and went up to her room saying, 'Oh, it slipped my mind, but I have a little something for you.'

Returning after a few seconds, she handed over a small gift box and cheerfully ordered. 'Go ahead, open it. Tell me if you like it.'

It was a beautiful pen and as I admired it she said, 'Uncle told me your exams are around the corner so I thought this will be of use. I hope you like it.'

'Of course, I do. It is lovely and just what I needed. Thank you so much, but you need not have bothered.'

'Don't be silly,' she gaily dismissed my protest. 'Now tell me what *you* have brought for me. I just love surprises.'

I didn't know how to react and holding the gift in my hand made it worse, but she didn't give up. 'Come on, hand it over. I can see you hiding something under your shirt.'

Before I could do anything, she stepped forward and laughing playfully tried to take out the book from under my shirt. We briefly jostled and the excitement made me a bit light-headed, but Jenny and Professor Hubertson were oblivious to my state and laughed aloud thoroughly enjoying themselves. Finally she stepped back and complained to her uncle. 'Rohan is teasing me. He has a gift for me, but is not giving it.'

'Rohan, it is very thoughtful of you to bring something for Jenny and you better give it to her now if you want to be left in peace. She doesn't give up easily.'

Caught in a fix I took out the gift I had brought for the professor and quietly handed it to her.

'Yippee!' she yelled excitedly. 'It's a book and I just love to read. Let's see which one this is.'

I watched embarrassed as she removed the wrapping paper and read aloud. 'It's the...*Complexities of Rare Elements...*' her voice trailed off and she gave me a puzzled look, but then recovered quickly. 'Just what I was looking for. Thanks, Rohan.'

Though it was discomfiting to remember my 'gift', we began chatting comfortably again and it soon felt I had known her all my life. I didn't feel like leaving at all but realizing I was overstaying my welcome, I thanked Professor Hubertson and said goodbye. To my surprise Jenny offered to walk with me to the bus stop, announcing to no one in particular. 'I want to stretch my legs.' It was a novel experience having a pretty girl by my side and even as I willed the bus be delayed, I felt life could not be more pleasurable. Alighting the bus, my eyes stayed glued on Jenny till she receded from my vision.

Jenny filled my thoughts completely. It was only when the evening shadows had lengthened and I was nearing my stop that it suddenly struck me that someone so beautiful must surely have a boyfriend. Moreover, I was sure I had ruined my chance by my embarrassing behaviour and made it worse with my gift. Surely, someone so stunning would be used to being showered with chocolates, flowers and perfumes. Not a book full of scientific jargon! I could imagine her setting the book on fire. My day was now ruined beyond redemption and I got down completely dispirited. I walked aimlessly for a long time before finally entering the dorm late at night to retire quietly, completely heartbroken.

In my turmoil there was no question of sleep; the opposite sex had so far inconsequentially occupied the periphery of my world yet this was now my only fascination. My love affair was sadly destined to fail even before it had begun.

'Rohan, are you awake?' a voice whispered in the dark.

It was John. Not inclined to converse I pretended to be asleep, but he persisted. 'Come on, you can't be sleeping already. I just saw you enter the dorm.'

When I still didn't reply, he shook my shoulder. 'It will be your loss if you don't answer.'

Eyes still shut, I pondered if this was a ploy and I hadn't quite made up my mind when he began walking away with a parting shot. 'I only wanted to know who Jenny is.'

Jenny! Sitting up instantly, I whispered urgently. 'Did you say Jenny?'

John returned with an impish smile and I pulled him down on my bed.

'So, that got your attention! But before I say anything, who is this girl?'

'I will tell you, but first tell me how did you hear of her?'

'Wow! You are so excited I may as well tell you. Around an hour back Hughes came to say there was a call for you and in your absence I went to take a message. The girl only asked me to tell you her name. Now, who is she?'

This development was beyond my wildest imagination and my heart beat excitedly even as I replied casually. 'Just someone I met at Professor Hubertson's. Really, nobody special.'

'Then why did she call?'

I quickly thought of an explanation. 'Probably because I forgot a paper the Professor gave me. He must have asked her to tell me so I wouldn't worry thinking I dropped it on the way.'

'Why didn't the professor call you?'

He doggedly tried to extract the maximum information, but anxious to savour this news I pretended to stifle a yawn. 'I am really sleepy. Thanks for the message. G'night.'

'Just one more question...' John persisted, but turning my back on him I closed my eyes and he retreated, muttering something under his breath.

As soon as John left, I became anxious to call Jenny, for it was killing me to find out why she had rung. Making sure no one was around I quietly got out of bed and stealthily slipped out of the dorm.

The hallway was deserted and with a thumping heart I dialed Professor Hubertson hoping he would not answer. The bell rang for a long time before I heard a sweet, 'Hello?' My prayer was answered, it was Jenny!

'Hi.'

'Who is it?'

'It's me.'

'Who is "me"? I don't know any *me*. Who do you wish to speak to?'

'It's me, Rohan.

'Hi, Rohan, it's so nice you called. I left a message.'

'Yes, you spoke to John. I hope it is not too late.'

'Not at all, though Uncle has retired.'

'OK. Please tell me why did you call?'

'Well, I just wanted to say sorry.'

'Sorry for what? In fact, *I* should be saying sorry for embarrassing you when you walked in.'

'That's fine. You were looking so sweet, tongue tied, and not knowing what to say or do. But why were you like that?'

'I will tell you when we meet next. Now, what are you sorry about?'

'Well, I know I can be a bit forward and I should not have forced you to give that gift to me. You obviously brought it for Uncle.'

'Well, actually I'm sorry for indeed I should have brought you something, but I didn't know I would meet you.'

'You mean you forgot I would be here today?'

'No, no, that's not what I meant. It just slipped my mind.'

'That is forgetting, is it not?'

'Come on, Jenny, don't be upset. I only meant you were very thoughtful to get me a gift while I wasn't. But I will make up the next time we meet.'

'No, you won't. I forbid you to get me anything. I quite like the one I forced out of you. I think it is a very special gift no girl has got before.'

'Please don't joke.'

'Seriously, I really like it. Maybe you can help me understand it.'

'Now you *are* joking!'

'Ha! Ha! I must rush now. Anyway, thanks for being so sweet. Goodnight.'

'Wait, Jenny. When do we meet again?'

'Why do you want to meet me?'

As I stumbled for a reply, Jenny said, 'I will be here this weekend but will come for a longer stay beginning next month. Why don't you come then? Uncle is a dear but it will be great to have someone my age to talk to.'

'That will be wonderful. I will certainly be there.'

'OK, see you then. Bye.'

'Bye, Jenny.'

I retired to bed with her voice still ringing in my ears. In the space of a short conversation I had climbed from the depths of despair to the heights of joy; there was hope and once again life felt worth living.

Jenny enveloped my thoughts like nothing else before. Realizing the impossibility of waiting a month to meet her I began scheming to see her or at the very least talk to her. The latter appeared more realistic and I concentrated on that.

Knowing she was at Rosemary School, I got a directory and noted the telephone number. The next step was tougher for I had to first make sure I was alone, but I managed that the same afternoon and rang up the number. Pretending to be a distant cousin I obtained Jenny's dorm number. I noted it carefully and kept it in my breast pocket. This slip of paper became my most precious possession, other than the pen she had gifted me.

For days I imagined what I would say to her, but unfortunately each time either someone else picked up the phone or I developed cold feet and disconnected immediately. Finally one day, I boldly asked for Jenny. I was put on hold and the waiting gave rise to panic. After what seemed like an eternity, I heard a 'Hello'. But despite careful planning I became dumbstruck. I could hear her voice on the other end repeating impatiently, 'Hello, who is it?' And then, after a final 'Helloooooooo' she disconnected the call.

I had messed up badly and spent considerable time reassessing my strategy and mustering courage. I finally decided to call over the weekend when she would be with the professor. At least then, if she came on line, as I hoped she would, I would have an excuse that I wished to talk to the professor.

The eagerly-awaited Saturday finally arrived and I impatiently waited till afternoon to make sure Jenny had reached. That was also when everyone would be out of the dorm, but due to an upcoming test I had reason to be indoors. Of course, John was suspicious, but thankfully he did not impose.

Finding the coast clear after lunch, I rushed to the telephone, praying fervently for Jenny to answer and she did! Ours was a short conversation.

'Hello,' said Jenny.

Well prepared, I spoke confidently. 'Hello, it's me, Rohan. Is that you, Jenny?'

'Hi Rohan, how are you?'

'I'm fine. And you?'

'Good. Wait a minute I'll give the phone to Uncle.'

'Wait!' I yelled, but it was too late. She had kept the receiver down and I cursed myself.

'Hello Rohan. How are you?' It was Professor Hubertson and I was ready with my speech.

'Very well, Sir. I just rang to say I received news from home and Professor Hardayal conveys his regards.'

'Thanks, when you reply please pass on my best wishes.'

'I will, Sir.'

'Rohan, if you are not doing anything special tomorrow why don't you come over? I have some papers you may find useful.'

I was yearning to hear that and replied enthusiastically. 'I am completely free. Is it OK if I reach by eleven?'

'Sure. Have lunch with us. See you then. Bye.'

'Bye, Sir.' I kept the phone down thoroughly pleased with the outcome. I would be seeing Jenny again!

The next day, I arrived wearing my best possible attire and Jenny was looking lovelier than ever. Though I scarcely knew her, it seemed humanly impossible to not love her. Thankfully, we got along very well; it may have helped that I brought her flowers though she insisted *Complexities of Rare Elements* occupied the pride of place on her bookshelf. Most importantly, I ensured to get her permission to call her at school and dutifully noted her number, though at that very moment, unknown to her, it lay in my pocket.

Over the next few months, Jenny and I spoke often and met almost every other weekend at Professor Hubertson's house. One day I mentioned our accidental meeting and she disclosed she was in the car with Professor Hubertson and had rushed in to pick up some papers that he had left behind. Of course, since she was with the Professor nobody asked her to sign in. On my part, I did not reveal how desperately I searched for her.

Time flew with Jenny's entry into my life. Weeks became months, then years, and I neared graduation. My stay was drawing to a close but it felt I had lived my entire life here. The place felt like home. It was only when someone asked my post-graduation plans or I received Bhai's letter that it struck me that I was to leave soon.

My love for Jenny knew no bounds and when she held my hand or hugged me I longed to kiss her and declare my love. But afraid to risk losing her, I held back. Moreover, Professor Hubertson was indulgent, but I was uncertain how he would react to this development so I made sure he had no hint of my romantic interest. Perhaps this was why Jenny too held back, though I was sure she loved me no less. These were difficult times as we found ourselves on an emotional roller coaster, despairing to commit but afraid to do so even as each new day was a cruel reminder of my impending departure, now only a few weeks away.

Gazing at Jenny's photograph for long hours, I tried to visualize life without her, each time realizing its impossibility. I could also not forsake Baoji, Ma and Bhai especially as they were under financial strain and needed me; Bhai now had two children and Baoji had retired.

One solution was to return home and come back for Jenny after getting a job. But this was fraught with agonizing possibilities, my family could object to me marrying a foreigner or Jenny could refuse moving to India especially as news of violent political clashes regularly filtered in. I struggled with this dilemma day and night and despaired for a way out.

With my thoughts constantly with Jenny and praying for a resolution to my predicament, I went through the motions of appearing for the final exams. Finally, the day arrived when, with a breaking heart, I booked my ticket; I simply had no alternative. That evening, with a heavy heart, I wrote to Baoji to inform him I was returning home.

'Hello, son,' said Professor Hubertson, pausing his weeding to look up, squinting from the bright sun falling into his eyes, as I entered, shutting the wooden gate behind me. 'What brings you here today? I thought we would now meet after your finals.'

Realizing the good professor could not have known I replied, 'Good morning, Professor. I should have rung before coming, but then thought I'd surprise you.'

'Well, it's a good surprise indeed and Jenny too will be happy you see you.'

'Is she here?' I asked, feigning ignorance. I thought she left last week.'

'You got your dates wrong, son.'

I nodded. 'Need help?'

'No son, but thanks for asking. It's too hot anyway. Why don't you go in and say hello to Jenny? I'll wash up and join you both.'

Thanking God that Professor Hubertson had not noticed, I quickly went into the living room and taking out the rose hidden inside my shirt smoothed its petals. I then called out softly. 'Jenny, it's me.'

As I looked up to her room, Jenny came downstairs slowly. Then wordlessly walking up to me, she hugged me tightly and began weeping, her entire body shaking in sorrow. We stood clenched in each other's arms for long, our hearts crying together at the prospect of separation till she finally released me and stepped back, wiped her eyes dry and smiled bravely. 'You are late and I began imagining what it would be like when you left.'

My heart breaking with the same thought, I replied unconvincingly. 'Don't feel sad, Jenny. I'll return very soon.'

Then spotting the flower in my hand she asked, 'What a lovely rose. Is it for me?'

I quickly thrust it at her. 'Of course, it is. Quick, take it before your uncle comes in.

Softly caressing the flower against her cheek, she asked, 'Why are you so scared of him? He is such a darling.'

'C'mon, even the faculty is scared of him, but I admit he has always been wonderful to me. Anyway, if he comes to know of my feelings for you I will surely be in deep trouble.'

'And how come *I* don't know about your feelings for me?' She asked, turning serious once more.

I fell silent, not knowing what to say and simply held her again. Just then the floorboards creaked and I pushed her away. 'Keep the rose in your room quickly.'

For all her bravado Jenny was just as scared of her uncle. She immediately rushed to her room while I quickly picked up a book and edged towards a chair.

'What happened, son?' asked Professor Hubertson, taking off his gloves. 'Didn't you call Jenny?'

'I did, Professor. She said she would be down right away.'

Settling into a sofa, Professor Hubertson bade me sit by his side. 'So, tell me, how are your finals going?'

'I hope to do well.'

'Good. I am glad you are here as there is something I want to discuss.'

'What is it, Professor?'

Just then Jenny came down and I stood to greet her, as if meeting her for the first time today. 'Hi. Nice to see you, I was under the impression you had left for college.'

'Good to see you too, Rohan,' Jenny replied, formally shaking my hand before sitting down. 'College opens next week, but I am not sure I will return.'

This was something new but before I could ask her, Professor Hubertson continued, 'Jenny, I was about to tell Rohan what I told you yesterday.'

Wondering whether Jenny's call last evening to see her urgently had anything to do with this, I turned to him.

'There has been a development since we last met that I disclosed to Jenny yesterday.'

'What is it, Professor?'

'Government has asked me to head an international project in Paris, in collaboration with scientists from the US, Canada and France. It's a very prestigious assignment. My only consideration was Jenny, as I can't possibly leave her alone. Fortunately, she is assured admission in an excellent college. We discussed this yesterday and Jenny is agreeable.'

Professor Hubertson's words struck me with numbing cruelty. Bewildered Jenny had agreed, I looked at her for an answer but she turned her eyes away. Then it struck me that I too was leaving shortly. My shoulders slumped as I helplessly grappled with the thought of being parted from her.

Professor Hubertson continued not noticing anything. 'Rohan, now listen carefully. I propose you join me at Paris after your finals. I can hire a few paid interns and you could be one of them. You could enroll for a Masters program alongside. You would get a head start in research and complete your studies as well. What do you think?'

Exhilarated at this life-saving offer to be with Jenny, I replied excitedly. 'This is wonderful! Under your guidance I will complete my research in no time.'

Upon hearing my reply, Jenny jumped up happily exclaiming a loud, 'Yes!' before suddenly becoming conscious

and sitting down abruptly. Amused at the excitement he had caused, Professor Hubertson looked at us adoringly even as Jenny and I could just not stop grinning.

Then a sobering thought struck me and it must have showed for Jenny immediately asked, 'What is it? You look concerned.'

'It's nothing at all.'

'C'mon tell us.'

'Well, I wouldn't have funds to travel to Paris.'

'Don't worry, Rohan,' said Professor Hubertson. 'I am sure we can adjust that against your stipend. And you can take tuitions to earn some extra money. I will arrange everything.'

I stayed until afternoon and as I took leave Jenny offered to walk with me to the bus stop, telling her uncle she had to pick something from the grocer. Just as we were out of sight she held my hand and snuggling up to me said softly, 'I am so happy it's working out for us. Wouldn't Paris be fun?'

During the ride back to the Academy I was in a state of bliss, time and again looking at Jenny's photograph. I was sure that after completing my research getting a job in India would be a certainty, which would be one step closer to spending the rest of my life with her. Things were once again looking up.

It was dusk when I reached the Academy. The dorm was noisy as usual, but I didn't feel like talking to anyone and retired after an early dinner. It had been a tiring but happy day and sleep came easy the moment I lay down.

Something woke me in the middle of the night and from my window I looked long at the waxing gibbous moon. Suddenly my thoughts traveled straight home, to Baoji, Ma and Bhai and I knew what disturbed me: I had completely forgotten about them while committing to move to Paris!

I lay awake struggling with my predicament. Moving to Paris would be unacceptable to Baoji and Ma, who were anxiously counting the days to my return. But by daybreak I convinced myself that since this move would translate into a better job back home, it would make them happy. I had been away for almost five years and felt sure another year would not matter that much. Though Jenny was constantly on my mind, I persuaded myself that she had not influenced my decision.

Dear Baoji, Ma and Bhai,

I am writing this hurriedly as I have to go for an exam. I wrote last time that I am coming back, but there has been some change in my plan. Professor Hubertson is moving to Paris (in France) and wants me to accompany him. He says this is an excellent opportunity to get invaluable research experience that will practically guarantee me a very good job. I have agreed after giving it considerable thought. I hope you will understand that this is important for my career. Postponing my return is disappointing, but it will be worth it in the long run. I will leave for Paris immediately after graduation and write to you on reaching there.

Love,

Rohan

Dear Rohan,

Your two letters were delivered together. As usual, they caused considerable excitement and I hurriedly opened one and Baoji, the other. Mine contained news of your arrival and as I read it aloud Ma happily thanked God her long wait was over.

But then Baoji read your other letter and from his expression we knew something was wrong.

We have been waiting so long for you and at first were very disappointed to learn of your new plans. Baoji had begun constructing a room for you and the first thing he did was to stop the work. For a few days he kept saying he should never have sent you abroad, but once I spoke to him, he understood you are merely postponing your return and is cheerful again. Even the work on your room has restarted so when you are back you will have your own room, something you always wanted. Ma too is sad but she is more practical and understands how important this is for you. We have waited many years and this additional time will also pass. So concentrate on your work and don't worry about us.

Maya and Baby Saket send their love; Baoji and Ma always say Saket is as naughty as you were!

Take good care and write immediately upon reaching Paris.

Love,

Bhai

With a lump in my throat I watched the receding shore of Sydney from Cunard Lines *Atlantis* taking me to Dover on the first leg of my journey to Paris. Graduation had been a grand affair and I received the Scholar Award for topping my class amidst thunderous applause. I had an offer to research at the Academy itself, but with Professor Hubertson and Jenny having left a month back I knew things would not be the same. Moreover, my friends were going their separate ways. Yet I felt sad leaving this wonderful city that sheltered me and made a man of me when I reached here a shaken, unsure youth.

John, Mark, Peter, Sanchu, Deep and all my other friends

came to see me off. Even Mr Hughes was present, carrying a home-baked cake. There was not a dry eye in the group when we hugged to say goodbye and promised to remain in touch.

A few days back, I had also visited Mr Fraser and Mike to bid them farewell. Now, as I turned to climb the gangplank I saw the good souls making their way to me. Seeing them made me feel like the chapter of my visit to Sydney was fittingly closing in the manner it had begun.

From the ship's deck I looked hard and long at the city that had been my home for so long, reliving all my experiences so that I never forgot them. Somehow in my sadness I was also dearly missing Baoji, Ma and Bhai as it felt exactly like when I had left Ambala. I knew from Bhai's letter that Baoji and Ma had not taken well to my move to Paris, but I was sure they would reconcile, consoling each other, as parents do, that it was for my good. At that moment I firmly promised myself I would be with them at the earliest opportunity. Looking at Jenny's photo I pictured returning home with her and immediately felt better.

Paris, France: 1923–1924

I somehow had a preconceived notion of Paris being no different from Sydney. But from the moment my train from Calais entered the city, I instinctively felt I would be proved completely wrong. I stepped down from the carriage to a warm welcome by Jenny looking lovelier than I could have possibly imagined, holding a bouquet of beautiful red roses for me. As we exited the station, French sounds wafted all around, adding to a charming foreignness. Later, we walked arm in arm amid other young couples on the Champs Elysees with colorful flowers in full bloom; there was romance in the air in this city of lovers.

I settled down easily as Professor Hubertson had arranged for everything in advance. My paying guest accommodation was a short walk to the laboratory I would work in and importantly it was near both the library where Jenny worked and her hostel; since Professor Hubertson traveled extensively, she found it convenient to stay independently near her workplace.

I soon discovered that if in the morning I left just half an hour early, I could meet Jenny, walk with her to the library, and still make it to my lab with five minutes to spare. I had the flexibility to leave once the day's work was done. Thus, I invariably found myself on the library steps waiting for the heavy wooden doors to open and Jenny merrily walk towards me. Thereafter, the evening was ours.

I soon became familiar with the lovely city; it was a fun-filled time as Jenny and I explored new places and identified favourite spots. On one such trip we made our way to *Le Lorraine*, a cozy restaurant at the corner of Boulevard Saint-Michel in the Latin quarter. Jenny had heard from a colleague that this was a favourite haunt of lovers, artists and students, in that order. Though the place was smoke-filled and crowded, seemingly not the perfect setting for romance, we soon became its regular patrons.

Le Lorraine was always full of young lovers mainly on account of a benign management that allowed a cup of coffee or a glass of cheap wine to be stretched indefinitely. Surprisingly this overcrowded place offered some of the most private moments to couples daring to occupy its candle-lit tables in darkened corners. This was because of an unwritten but highly respected rule that this sterile, comparatively cleaner and greatly discrete area was reserved for young couples. Once a couple settled down, a waiter would take their order of coffee or wine and sometimes a snack, and after having served them leave them alone. A few hours later the couple would leave, the girl briefly adjusting her dress, and the waiter would find a significant tip left for him.

Jenny and I always sat with the artists and students around a bar in the middle of the room, hearing them debate late into the evening while blowing cheap cigarette smoke rings and drinking vodka. Our attention was, however, on the enticing shadowed periphery, but we were not bold enough to cross the Rubicon.

Our trips to the restaurant soon became an exercise in self-restraint. Finally, we stopped tempting ourselves and began spending our evenings in open parks. In hindsight I believe that the testing times at *Le Lorraine* marked the maturing of our relationship.

❧

I intuitively knew it would be a perfect day; a brilliant morning like none before it. Nature was at its invigorating best and indeed life felt worth living.

Picking up Jenny's photograph from a side table and looking upon her lovely face I savoured the beautiful memories of the day gone by. I loved her immeasurably from the day I had first seen her and I finally knew she reciprocated with all her heart!

❧

The previous evening had been unplanned and for that reason utterly romantic as it unfolded. Professor Hubertson was away to Canada and after work I met Jenny and we took a leisurely walk. There was a slight nip in the air and as others hurried indoors it felt wonderful to just aimlessly walk about, oblivious to the hustle and bustle around us. With the evening deepening the streets emptied, except for a few avant-garde painters and poets in park corners with their small bands of fans.

We first went towards the park and then I steered Jenny to *La Brasserie,* a few streets away, a frightfully expensive restaurant well known for its incomparable dining experience for a price far beyond my modest stipend. However, I had been planning this special day for long and buttressed my resources with a few teaching assignments.

I swiftly guided a surprised Jenny up its sweeping stairs into the heavily carpeted lobby, past the formidable impeccably suited doorman whose penetrating eyes seemed to count each of my 34 Francs with disdain. He thankfully kept his peace, distracted, no doubt, by the big tip handed in by a departing patron and we entered without embarrassment, the huge glass doors softly closing behind us.

In its hushed environs the place was luxurious beyond my wildest imagination. The brocaded tapestry and thick, soft, multi-colored rugs and golden chandeliers bathed everyone in a rich glow. Soft music filled the air and smartly-uniformed waiters courteously attended to the *crème de la crème* of French society waiting to be ushered into the dining area. Even as I gaped, Jenny dragged me to one side and whispered anxiously. 'What do you think you are up to?'

Somewhat recovering composure, I replied with practiced ease but in a whisper in deference to where we stood. 'Why, dear, what is the matter? This is a wonderful place. You'll like it.'

'But how can you afford it?'

'It's no problem. I have lots of money.'

'Don't be a fool. I know exactly how much money you make. Let's go to our usual café in the park.'

As she spoke, I felt the doorman's eyes boring into me and fearing his intervention, I desperately pleaded with Jenny in hushed tones that money was not an issue. But she was unmoved and brushing aside my arguments declared firmly. 'Well, I am leaving and waiting outside. You can either join me or eat here alone.' And before I could open my mouth she resolutely stepped out of the restaurant, smiling pleasantly at the doorman as he opened the door for her.

Nonplussed, I tried to appear engrossed in the paintings around me but racked my brain on how to handle this unforeseen situation. After a few minutes, realizing I had no option, I exited red-faced, avoiding the doorman's eyes as he opened the door with an exaggerated bow, smirking at my discomfiture.

With both enthusiasm and ego deflated and the evening doomed, I slowly walked to Jenny who was standing at the street corner. But strangely this diversion had perked her up and gaily pulling my arm and running her fingers through my hair she said, 'You are so sweet, wanting to spend all your hard earned money on me. Come on, tonight's dinner is on me.'

A few people were about the streets at this time of the evening and as we walked holding hands with Jenny chatting cheerfully, my mood improved. It undoubtedly helped that in my heart I knew I could little afford the expensive evening I had planned. After a while we sat down on a nearby bench.

'So, Rohan, have you decided what to do once you complete your research?'

'Professor Coulomb wants me to help him in his project.'

'But what about a proper job?'

'I am sure I can get good teaching or research assignments here.'

'And will you go back to India then?'

'Yes, I have to. In fact, Bhai is now insisting that I should return immediately. I have been away far too long.'

'But do you *want* to go back?'

'Of course, I have told you before that I must go back, but I have not planned exactly when.'

Jenny would invariably become somber whenever our conversation veered towards my return to home, but today she shot back combatively. 'Will you get a job there as good as one here? I hear that unless you are an Englishman you don't even get a job in India. There is also so much violence there.'

'That is not true,' I countered. 'There are plenty of jobs there and Ambala is perfectly safe.'

'You *know* that is not a fact.'

'OK I concede the job situation is not great, but it will surely improve. Besides, my family is waiting for me.'

'I understand that, but what about me?'

'You know I love you, Jenny.'

'You only *say* that, but you want to leave me. Why don't you go back immediately then? Stop wasting my time and leave me alone!'

Jenny suddenly got up and began walking away rapidly. Surprised by her outburst I ran after her yelling, 'Jenny, wait!'

When I caught up with her, she was crying quietly and not sure what to do, I simply held her hand and guided her to another nearby bench. I wiped her tears and asked softly, 'Please, Jenny. People are watching. Why are you crying? What has happened to you today?'

She sat silently for a few minutes and then turned towards me and looked deep into my eyes. As I tried to fathom how she felt, she cupped my face in her soft hands and slowly bringing me closer whispered, 'I love you.' Hardly had her words registered when she leaned forward and kissed me tenderly. I could feel the gentleness of her lips, the saltiness of her tears, and the warmth of her love as she kept crying softly and kissing me passionately.

Oblivious to passing pedestrians, we abandoned ourselves to each other. Ever since we had first met I had often dreamed of kissing her, but that was incomparable to what I now felt. Her passion was tinged with a desperation I could not have imagined possible and a sadness I did not fully comprehend. I had always imagined my first kiss would be a happy, romantic moment, but I now learned love and sadness combine to make a more fatal emotion, little understood and never forgotten.

I know not how long we sat or when we started walking holding each other tightly, but unaware of the route we took or people we passed we found ourselves at her doorstep where unable to part, shielded by darkness, we kissed for long till someone opened the door and Jenny quickly disengaged from me and slipped inside. As I did each time, I said, 'I love you,' and for the first time she replied, 'Me too,' before blushing and closing the door.

I stood transfixed for a long time before slowly turning away. During the walk back I tried to recall all that had happened, but somehow the only memories that remained were the softness of her lips and the scent of her perfume.

Smiling at the recollection of the day gone by I kept her photograph down and got dressed after a hurried bath, wearing my favorite shirt that Jenny had gifted me on my last birthday. We usually fixed our next meeting before parting, but having made no such arrangement last evening I decided to meet her at the tram stop outside her hostel.

Rushing to Jenny I began wondering how, with our kisses fresh in mind, she would respond; she was prim and proper with no previous liaisons with boys and things had happened so spontaneously I was unsure of her reaction on this new day. After about a half hour of impatiently scanning her hostel door, Jenny exited, looking ravishing in a pink skirt and blouse. As she began to briskly walk towards her library, I ran behind her. 'Jenny, wait.'

Surprised to see me, she stopped in her tracks, blushing when I came closer. 'What are you doing here? I am late.'

'I just had to see you. Let me walk with you.'

'Don't you have a morning class?'

'There's still time.'

We walked on in silence; she seemed somewhat changed, quieter, withdrawn and was avoiding looking directly at me.

Fearing I had upset her in some way I hesitatingly asked, 'What happened, dear? Are you fine?'

'Of course,' she replied before relapsing into a studied silence even as we continued walking side by side.

After a few minutes, realizing we were already near the library, I desperately held her hand and asked. 'Are you upset about yesterday?'

Jenny softened. 'Don't be silly. I am not upset. It's just that things happened so fast and I don't know where it will lead. I am so afraid.'

She looked so helpless that I wanted to hug her tight but said simply. 'Don't be frightened. I will always be with you.'

Jenny smiled and touching my cheek softly ran inside the library without a word. At that moment I knew I needed to commit for there was no way I could hurt her.

I reached the library much before closing time, buying Jenny's favorite flowers on the way. The tower clock struck six and when Jenny stepped outside I was relieved to see an expectant look on her face knowing it could only be me she searched for. Sure enough, the moment she saw me she came rushing with a charming smile.

'Hi, I am so glad to see you. These flowers are lovely!'

'I had to come because you rushed away in the morning without even saying bye.'

Jenny did not react and seemingly lost in thought began to walk on even as I stepped in besides her. Some moments later, she turned to me. 'Please forget this morning. Let us have coffee.'

Her changing moods were disturbing and I persisted. 'But what happened? I only want to know if I hurt you in any way.'

'Don't be silly. I'm absolutely fine, dear,' replied Jenny holding my hand but when she continued walking quietly I asked again. 'Please tell me what is troubling you?'

'Rohan,' sighed Jenny, releasing my hand, her troubled eyes betraying her tension. 'Uncle called yesterday.'

'What did he say? When is he returning?'

'That is the problem. He says he has to stay longer and wants me to join him immediately.'

Even before she completed her sentence, I felt a rising desperation. 'But how can this be? I mean, he has his project here. He just can't stay there!'

'You know he is in Ottawa to assist Canadian colleagues on the same project. They are on the verge of a breakthrough and he needs to be there now.'

'How long does he expect it to take?'

'He doesn't know for sure. He feels it may take a year.'

'You can surely stay here, why must you go to Ottawa?'

'Well, Uncle knows you are moving back to India and I guess he would much rather have me with him than be here alone.'

'This doesn't make sense. Professor Hubertson can't travel all over the world like this and make you do the same.'

'Be reasonable, Rohan. You know very well he is all the family I have and by asking me to join him in Ottawa he is thinking only of me, not himself.'

'I know, dear, but I came to Paris only because of you. What will I do here if you go away?'

'You could come to Ottawa, can't you?'

'I can't leave my work when it's about to finish in a few months. I have also been away from home for so long and my parents expect me back now.'

'I guess there is nothing to say then. You have to go back to India and I can't disappoint Uncle.'

'Don't say that, please. I am confident things will work out for us. You know I have a few job offers here and McAllister Labs is considering placing me in their Delhi office in India. This way we could settle in India and if you don't like it there we have the option to come back anytime.'

'Rohan, there is so much violence in India against British rule. It is not at all safe.'

'That's not true. Delhi is very safe besides with my job we will live like royalty.'

'Oh Rohan, too many things are happening all at once and I am confused.'

'Just know that if you go to Canada it will be difficult for us to be together.'

'I can't bear the thought of being away from you.'

'Then you must tell your uncle about us.'

'Yes, but not over phone. I shall tell him in person and I am sure he will help me take the right decision.'

My shoulders slumped as I realized her mind was made. 'So, when are you leaving?'

'Uncle said he would send the ticket. I guess it should be a month from now.'

Jenny left for Canada after exactly twenty-four days, each minute of which is imprinted in my mind with unreal clarity. We were two lovers being torn apart by circumstances beyond control and while we outwardly pretended this was a temporary parting, there was a lurking fear we might never see each other again.

An unknown and frightening future loomed and there was no easy solution. Professor Hubertson could simply put his foot down on the prospect of Jenny moving to India, especially since she herself wasn't sure of it. On the other hand, I couldn't imagine living abroad for the rest of my life, away from Baoji, Ma and Bhai. Also, though I kept this apprehension to myself, Baoji and Ma were too conservative to accept a 'foreign' daughter-in-law. I was torn between my family and Jenny and the thought of one without the other was heart breaking. While in academics I could easily find solutions to the most complex problems, real life had me stumped.

Thus, Jenny and I met daily, desperately spending each waking moment together before grudgingly parting late at night. Those unforgettable days were full of high emotions with a surfeit of tears, smiles, sorrow, laughter, but above all pure love, fierce and passionate.

It was the evening before Jenny's departure and my anxiety was growing by the minute with the possibility of losing her forever. Then, drifting on a boat in the shadow of the Eiffel I silently asked Baoji and Ma to forgive me for my trespass, and holding Jenny's hand in mine asked, 'Will you marry me, my love?'

She looked at me for long, her eyes brimming with tears before whispering a barely audible, 'Yes,' and kissing me.

Later, we walked hand in hand on Champs Elysees and long after the city had slept reached her hostel when for the first time, by unspoken arrangement, she broke the house rule. Holding my hand she let me furtively into her room. It was dark, but we did not need light and guided by our hearts made the most beautiful love, my first time and hers. There was a slight chill in the air when I carefully exited her room at dawn and made my way out undetected.

I felt the world at large would instantly know the happenings of the night before, and walked fast not daring to meet anyone's eyes. But when people walked right past without a second glance, I had a doubt: had I dreamt everything? Daytime seemed to render the previous night's passion unreal.

When I reached, Jenny was already outside, her suitcase ready by her side. With last night's encounter fresh in mind I felt awkward and she too averted her eyes as I picked up her suitcase and we silently began walking towards Gare d'Orsay from where she would embark on the first leg of her long journey.

I stopped after some time and, putting down her suitcase, held her hand and looked deep into her eyes. Then, taking out of my pocket a ring Ma had given me, I slipped it on her finger with trembling hands. For what seemed an eternity she looked at the ring and then, as if resolving something, her face lit up and with a radiant smile she slipped her hand into mine. I knew without an iota of doubt that she would be back for me and everything seemed perfect again.

After Jenny's departure I began working day and night on my project, grabbing only a few hours of sleep at the lab itself, knowing upon its completion I could return home to seek Baoji and Ma's permission to marry Jenny. After that, I planned to ask Jenny to visit India along with Professor Hubertson for the wedding and then return to Paris till I landed a job back home.

It seemed like the perfect plan especially when I was offered a job, and upon learning of my visit to India they agreed to hold the spot for me till I returned. That very day I wrote to Baoji informing him I would be home in two months. Realizing some things are better explained in person I purposely did not mention either the job or Jenny.

Jenny and I spoke daily on phone, the distance

strengthening our longing to be together again. She had yet to disclose our relationship to Professor Hubertson and upon my insistence promised to do so right away.

The professor's approval was crucial and all afternoon I anxiously awaited her call; he loved me like a son, but he was getting on in age and I feared he might not agree to Jenny moving so far away to India. Even as dusk fell and I nervously paced the room, the phone remained ominously silent. And when I desperately tried her number the line just kept ringing. Finally, I fell into a fitful sleep.

It was past midnight when the shrill ring of the phone jarred me awake and I leaped across the room to grab it. 'Jenny?'

It was indeed Jenny and she sounded as if a child, shaken and scared. 'I am sorry to wake you, but I just had to speak with you.'

I almost shouted in alarm, 'What happened, Jenny? Is everything all right?'

There was a brief pause after which she could hold back no more. She cried uncontrollably while I tried to console her without knowing the reason, imagining the worst. 'Jenny, please listen, calm down. Everything will be all right. What happened? Where is your uncle?'

Finally, she quietened with considerable effort and through sniffles replied, 'I am calling from the hospital, Uncle had a heart attack.'

'When! How did it happen? Is he alright?'

'He is fine now, but it gave me such a fright.'

'Were you with him when it happened?'

'Yes. It was around eleven. Thank God the ambulance reached quickly and he received immediate attention. Doctors say he is out of danger now.'

'I am so relieved to hear that. You had me really worried. Please do convey my best wishes when you see him.'

'I will get to see him in a few minutes. He will be happy to hear from you. In fact, just yesterday he even spoke to Professor Coulomb to find out about your work.'

'He is too kind.'

'Yes, he is wonderful. I thank God I am here with him now. I would never have forgiven myself had something happened to him while he was alone.'

'Don't worry, nothing will happen to him.'

'I must go now, Rohan. I am feeling so much better after speaking to you. I'll call you again tomorrow.'

This was hardly the time to speak of our plans and I wasn't sure how this development would affect our future; the uncertainty was worrisome.

I called her the next morning, relieved she answered at the first ring.

'Hello.'

'Hi Jenny.'

'Rohan, I am so glad you called. I just entered and instantly knew it was you.'

'How is Professor Hubertson today?'

'Much better, but the doctors say his heart is damaged and recovery will be slow at his age. It seems the problem began long back and somehow remained undetected. But they are hopeful that with good nursing he should be alright.'

'That is good news indeed.'

'Yes, I am so happy. He has taken it well and plans to cut down on his work.'

'Good. When he is better, both of you should come here.'

'That is a problem. I asked the doctors about his going to Paris and they strictly advised against any travel for at least six months.'

'Do you think he can manage on his own when you come back?'

'Rohan, how can you even think I will leave him in this condition? I must be with him till he improves.'

'Hold on, Jenny. What about our plans? I have already written home. And what about your job here?'

'Tell me what I should do, Rohan? Should I leave him when he needs me the most?'

'Of course not, but...'

'I have been thinking of this all day. I want to be with you, but I will never forgive myself if I were to leave him now.'

'You are right. Let us calmly decide what we should do.'

'I will speak to his doctors tomorrow for their final assessment. Uncle was fine today and I hope they may yet clear him for travel. If yes, I am sure he will want to go home to Sydney and we can all return with him.'

'OK. I will wait for your call. Please take care of yourself. Bye, I love you.'

'I love you, too.'

Things were certainly not going according to plan and I anxiously waited for Jenny's call the next day. Finally, at around 8 p.m., soon after dinner, the phone rang and I grabbed the receiver.

'Hi Jenny, how is the professor.'

'I am afraid it's not good news. They ran some tests and found his heart is badly affected by the stroke. They say medicine can only slow further damage but not reverse it. However, they say that with good care he can live long. I am so afraid, Rohan. I wish you were here with me.'

I could hear her weeping softly and my heart was breaking that I was so far and could not comfort her. 'Don't cry, Jenny.

Professor Hubertson is strong and will definitely be fine. How long will he remain in hospital?'

'They are discharging him tomorrow.'

'Does he know how bad it is?'

'Yes, he insisted and the doctors told him everything. After hearing them he asked only one question, whether he can travel to Sydney and they said yes but after six months of rest and therapy. He was quiet for a long time and then began writing at length and after finishing asked one of the doctors to sign as a witness before giving it to me for safekeeping. Rohan, he has written his will and left everything to me, and an endowment to the Academy. I sensed this relieved him, but I couldn't help but cry.'

'Don't worry, he will recover soon.'

'I certainly pray he does. He is all I have.'

'That's not true, you have me too, Jenny.'

'Of course, yes. And one more thing, I told Uncle about us.'

'You did! Quick, what did he say?'

'He was very happy and advised we settle down soon; I think he realizes he does not have much time. Since he cannot travel, he said that you should come here and he will get you a permanent job in his project.'

'Wait! I already have a job offer here and am only waiting for your return.'

'Rohan, I just told you I cannot leave Uncle. By the way, he has decided to move nearer to the project site and we shall be seeing a house this weekend.'

'But you can't live there! What about your job?'

'It's a small township and Uncle has confirmed there is a vacancy for me in its library. I really wish you would understand that I must be with him till he is well and if you come we can all be together.'

'Wait! Instead of returning home I moved to Paris from Sydney and now you are asking me to move even further away to Canada!'

'It is only for a short time till Uncle can travel.'

We debated at length, discussing various options to be together but finding no easy answers. I knew I could not forsake her but I desperately wished to avoid moving further away from Baoji and Ma. I pleaded for her to return even as my mind accepted she could not leave Professor Hubertson at this juncture. There was no meeting ground between longing and reality.

Finally, physically and emotionally drained, she said, 'Please think calmly. I am only asking you to come temporarily to Canada and once Uncle is well we will all return together. You can even go meet your parents before coming here.'

'But what if he can't travel even after a few months?'

'Then we will stay here till he is fit to do so.'

'But that may take a year!'

'Yes, it may indeed but we should hope for the best.'

'OK Jenny, I guess you are right. We'll speak tomorrow. Do convey my best to the professor.'

'Bye, Rohan. I love you.'

'I love you, too. Goodnight.'

I kept the phone down slowly, trying to grapple with this new situation. I understood Jenny could not possibly leave her uncle in his present condition so I had two options: return home and hope she would join me after a few months or join her now till we could journey home together. Both options rested on Professor Hubertson's quick recovery.

Jenny's parting words rang in my head all evening and my decision was made by bedtime: I loved her too much to bear being parted. Thinking throughout of their disappointment, I penned a letter informing Baoji and Ma that I had postponed my return by about six months as my work necessitated going to Canada. As I sealed the letter, I vowed to make it up to them by spending the rest of my life caring for them.

Glendale, Ontario: 1924–1925

On 14 January 1924, I reached Ottawa in the midst of a blustering snowstorm. Straining hard for a glimpse of Jenny, I was relieved to finally spot her waving to me from behind a glass partition in the Immigration and Customs area. She was enveloped in a large down coat, snowflakes clinging to her, holding a bouquet of red roses. As she dashed forward, hugging me tightly and melting against me, I knew I had made the correct decision; I could not possibly live without her.

The roads were clogged and we waited out the storm, sipping hot coffee in a cafeteria. Holding her hand, my tiredness vanished as she excitedly briefed me on Professor Hubertson's recovery and her new job. Then she teased, 'I am sure you have forgotten the name of the town where we are staying?'

'Not at all! How far is it from here?' I replied, straining to recall the name she had told me half a dozen times; I was always poor at remembering names of places and people.

'About a four-hour drive, but it may take longer because of the snow. Come on, admit you don't remember the name.'

'But I do, it begins with a "G". It's Gandle...?'

'Ha! Ha! I knew you wouldn't remember, but you are pretty close. It's a beautiful town, Glendale.'

'Glendale,' I repeated, trying its sound myself.

For a few cozy hours, we caught up on lost time before the snowstorm subsided and we began our journey to Glendale in a spacious Auburn Brougham, which Jenny explained was hired for Professor Hubertson till he recovered.

It was slow going on the slushy road, but we soon left the city behind for a desolate countryside. As far as I could see, there was nothing else but heavy snow on both sides of the long winding road; it appeared we were slowly but surely entering deeper and deeper into a narrowing white tunnel.

It was comforting to feel Jenny's hand in mine, but I had a sudden, strong longing for the heat of a big, bright yellow Indian sun on my face, to look into its blinding glare till compelled to squeeze my eyes shut and look away. A sudden brake jolted me back to reality and I reassured myself that ours would be a short stay here. Little did I know that destiny had other plans that were unfolding at that very moment.

Jenny led me up the driveway of her new home, a quaint townhouse with shingled roof and over a dozen pines and maples in its front yard, all thickly snow-covered. Even though she repeatedly assured me Professor Hubertson was happy for us, I was nervous since this was our first meeting after him being in the know of our relationship. But my misgivings vanished the moment the door opened and Professor Hubertson, looking shockingly weak, welcomed me warmly. It was soon like old times as we caught up with each other over coffee.

Professor Hubertson's passion was palpable as he eagerly explained how close he was to a breakthrough. 'Rohan, I *know* it will happen soon, another six months at the outer limit and we would have identified the isotope. Can you contemplate its implication?'

'That will be great Professor,' I replied dutifully. 'I am positive you will succeed soon.'

'Yes, I *must* succeed,' replied Professor Hubertson determinedly before adding somberly, 'You probably know I don't have much time left.'

'Don't say that, Uncle,' protested Jenny. 'The doctors say you will recover completely. You should not think negatively.'

'Yes Sir,' I added. 'You will be perfectly well soon.'

Professor Hubertson suddenly got up. 'Don't worry, children, I will be fine. Dear, Rohan must be tired after the long journey. Please take him to his room so he can rest.'

Professor Hubertson had got me appointed as his assistant and I was to stay with him and Jenny till the end of the month. Thereafter, I would move to a rented room nearby, which suited me fine for I planned to be here for not more than six months.

Jenny took me around Glendale—a tiny township with one school, a hospital, a cluster of shops, and a beautiful public library at which she worked. Within a few days I was familiar with the roads and places and friendly neighbours began to acknowledge me.

Professor Hubertson's lab was a few miles outside town and it was a lovely drive in his office car that picked us up each morning and dropped us back after work; the car was a privilege, but obviously required in view of his ill health.

As I worked alongside him, I discerned his feverish urgency and sadly realized that he obviously sensed his time was limited. He was like a father to me and I vowed to spare no effort to help him complete his task.

There was a marked maturing of my relationship with Jenny as we settled into a routine in a domestic environment, practically under one roof. I only slept in my room at night and spent all my time at Professor Hubertson's, including having meals there. His approval of my relationship with Jenny was evident, though he chose not to broach the subject.

It was sheer joy to explore the town with Jenny or simply be together, hand in hand, basking in the warmth of a fireplace in the living room, long after Professor Hubertson had retired for the night. During these moments we would discuss future plans and renew our commitment despite still being unsure when and how to start the journey.

We were physically comfortable, but Jenny strongly felt against betraying her uncle's trust and I respected her decision. The passion of our one-night tryst in Paris was not repeated.

With the passage of time I became anxious to marry Jenny with the blessings of Baoji, Ma and Bhai. But that would be possible only when we went home and I knew she would not accompany me unless we were married. I wrestled with this dilemma day and night.

Professor Hubertson suffered a second heart attack on a quiet evening while having tea after an exhausting day at work. We had just run a few tests at work, but the results were somewhat disappointing. As we relaxed, I happened to glance at the professor and noticed his face suddenly turn pale.

'Don't worry, Professor. I will review the tests to find out what went wrong. I'm sure it's only a minor issue.'

Professor Hubertson did not reply and the next moment Jenny and I watched him labour to get up, as if in slow motion. He almost managed to stand when, before we could react, he suddenly cried aloud, falling back into his chair, pain writ large over his face that was now chalk white.

'Uncle!' shouted Jenny, dropping her teacup and rushing to him. I too got up quickly at the same time helplessly shouting, 'Quick, his medicine. Call the doctor!'

It was a chaotic few minutes as Professor Hubertson lay with closed eyes, hand on his heart, gasping for breath while Jenny desperately waved smelling salts under his nose and I vigorously massaged his hands. After a few more panic stricken moments he seemed to relax and though still very pale, colour appeared to slowly return to his cheeks. Opening his eyes, he whispered weakly, 'Don't worry. I am fine.'

Jenny was in tears when the doctor came, gave Professor Hubertson an injection, placed him on a stretcher and strapped an oxygen mask on his face. As the ambulance sped to the hospital, she held her uncle's hand throughout and I sat by her side knowing it would break her heart if anything happened to him.

Professor Hubertson fortunately recovered and looked his normal self by night as he consoled a still distraught Jenny, 'Dear, don't worry so much. Nothing will happen to me. And Rohan is here with you.'

During Professor Hubertson's stay at the hospital, I laboured desperately to conclude his work successfully as a way to say 'thank you' for all he had done for me. I also knew this was the only way for us to go back home at the earliest.

On the tenth day of Professor Hubertson's hospitalization, Jenny rang me at the lab to inform he would be home by the time I returned. I had run a few crucial tests and was anxiously awaiting the results, all the while imagining the professor's happiness when they vindicated his work.

It was dusk when, completely exhausted, I sat at the

professor's desk with my tabulations and his notes in hand, carefully analyzing data from the tests. As I looked at my final calculations, a chill enveloped me and the discovery hit me hard, like a fist in the middle of my stomach, draining me of all energy as the papers slipped out of my unfeeling fingers to the floor. I had just confirmed the unimaginable: Professor Hubertson, amongst the greatest scientists of his time, was completely wrong!

I rechecked the results a hundred times but came to the same conclusion each time: the project was doomed to failure. I had irrefutable proof that Professor Hubertson and his team's hard work over the years, here, in Paris, and Sydney was an utter waste. But knowing his broken heart would not withstand the shock, I could not possibly break this news to him. I needed time and, before entering home, decided to play a charade till he was strong enough to bear the disappointment.

'Come on in, Rohan,' Jenny called cheerfully when I let myself in. 'You are awfully late and Uncle has been asking for you ever since he came back.' Then looking closely at me she asked, 'Is everything alright? You look as if you have seen a ghost.'

'Everything is fine, dear. I am just tired. How is Professor Hubertson doing?'

'He is resting, but you can see him. He looks good.'

Going up to Professor Hubertson's room I knocked and entered to find him reading a magazine. 'Welcome home, Professor, you look good.'

'I feel very good. I am afraid I gave you kids a fright, but I feel perfect now and am looking forward to going back to the lab.'

My heart sank but I gamely replied, 'Of course, everyone is keenly awaiting your return.'

'Come, Rohan,' said Jenny, coming up behind me. 'Let Uncle rest.'

'Yes, that's right,' I replied, turning to leave. 'Good night, Professor. I'll look you up tomorrow.'

The next few months were hectic and emotionally trying. After being medically cleared to resume work, Professor Hubertson accompanied me to the lab each day and I worked by his side knowing full well its futility, but not daring to disclose the truth. Yet, I knew it was only a matter of time when he himself discovered the inevitable reality. I shuddered to think of its effect.

I was sure his long illustrious career would have been peppered with a few setbacks, but I feared at this stage of life and given his fragile health he would not be able to overcome what would undoubtedly be his greatest disappointment. I felt it was my responsibility to be with him at that critical time, if only to console him, but a part of me also wished to be far away when that happened.

One day when Professor Hubertson was in his study, I broached the topic of my return home with Jenny. 'Dear, it's almost six months now that I have been here and Professor Hubertson's work is still not done. What do you think?'

'You would know better, when do *you* think it will finish?'

I replied carefully. 'Well, I have some idea, but he undoubtedly knows better. He feels he is close, but it may be some time before he finds the truth.'

Jenny laughed. 'That's very illuminating! Anyway, what is in your mind?'

'I was thinking of going home.'

Sensing my anxiousness Jenny became quiet, and then as if making up her mind she replied, 'I guess you must go if you really have to. I understand you have been away so long and miss your family and I will miss you a lot when you are away.'

'Is there no way you can accompany me'" I asked hopefully, though in my heart I already knew her reply.

'Who will look after Uncle if I do?'

'I understand, but India is so far and I want you with me.'

'Then surely you must come back at the earliest.'

'Yes, I will, but if you count the journey time it shall be at least four months till I return.'

'That's so long! What will I do? I wish you wouldn't go.'

We talked late into the night long after Professor Hubertson retired, discussing our future even as we despaired to make sense of our situation. Jenny brought wine that we sipped slowly and unknowingly the minutes became hours and we lay silently on the soft carpet, holding each other, having given up on unravelling our complications.

Maybe it was the wine or the suppressed memory of our last time together in Paris or simply our passion and desperation, but Jenny's resolve and my self-control were forgotten. It was dawn when I silently slipped out of the house and hurried through the desolate roads to my room.

After many marathon discussions with Professor Hubertson and Jenny, I booked my tickets to go home to obtain Baoji and Ma's approval for the marriage and return to Glendale. Professor Hubertson expected to complete his work in six to eight months and we agreed we would travel together to Ambala for the wedding. Thereafter, he would go on to Sydney and Jenny and I would take a final call on where to settle, in India or Sydney. I was, of course, confident that once she met my family she would agree our future lay in Ambala.

The only hitch I foresaw, which I kept to myself, was Professor Hubertson's expectation of completing the project, which according to me was impossible. I only feared unforeseen complications this could create but, despite misgivings, the mere thought of being home was enough to bring cheer and I immediately dashed off a letter to Baoji intimating my travel plans.

I remember the day distinctly. It was very sunny and a fresh breeze caressed our faces as Jenny and I chose gifts for Baoji and Ma. Only fifteen days were left for my departure, but firming up our wedding plans made the temporary parting bearable. Done with shopping, I picked up a coffee for Professor Hubertson as Jenny and I held hands and slowly walked home when I told her for the umpteenth time. 'You are looking so radiant it's as if you are keeping a wonderful secret.'

Jenny laughed aloud. 'You know I have no secrets from you.'

'But it seems you are not telling me something.' Affectionately touching her cheeks and pulling her closer I teased, 'Is it that you are happy I am going?'

'Don't be ridiculous, Rohan,' chided Jenny, suddenly serious.

'Come, dear. I was just joking.'

We walked on in silence and as I wondered how to bring her back to her usual cheerful self, she suddenly stopped and said, 'Rohan, can we sit in the park for some time, please?'

'Yes, of course. Do tell me what is the matter, dear. I don't like it when you are so quiet.'

We entered the park and sat near a few kids playing on the

swings. I waited for her to say something but she was quiet, looking intently at the playing children and I commented. 'Is it not wonderful to be a child and enjoy life without worries.'

'Yes,' Jenny spoke thoughtfully, still gazing at the children. 'But since one can not be a child forever surely the next most wonderful thing must be to have a child.'

'Yes, of course.'

And then Jenny turned and looking straight at me said calmly. 'I am pregnant.'

'That's not possible!'

'What do you mean?' she retorted, bewildered and pained.

I digested the news silently, trying to fathom its implication even as Jenny slowly withdrew her hand from mine, tears forming in her beautiful eyes. Regretting my insensitivity, I cupped her face in my hands and kissed her softly. 'Thank you dear. You have made me the happiest person in the world. I love you.'

Jenny relaxed and now crying silent tears of love kissed me back. At that moment I vowed to always be by her side and to never again let her feel helpless.

We sat in the park till dusk had fallen only to realize it had emptied and we were alone. 'Come, sweetheart,' I whispered softly. 'Let us go home. I am afraid Professor Hubertson's coffee is now cold, but the news shall surely cheer him up.'

'But we can't tell him! He would know we betrayed his trust.'

'If you say so, but we must certainly get married soon.'

'What about your folks? Will they be happy?'

I had not thought of that and instantly realized that this development would cause a big scandal at home, but knowing Jenny would not understand I simply assured her. 'Don't worry. Let us go now.'

With her words still ringing in my mind I continued

walking in a daze, unable to fully grasp what was happening but knowing her simple words had in an instant changed my life completely. Glancing sideways it was unreal to comprehend this frail girl was having a baby...my baby, but it was true!

She appeared unchanged, but looking again at her striding silently besides me, it was clear that somehow, somewhere, unnoticed, she had altered deeply and was no longer the girl I had loved so long. She was giving me the most precious gift a woman could offer and I felt proud of being loved by her. Just before entering the house, Jenny wiped her face clear of signs of tears, fixed her hair, gave me an encouraging smile and once again looked her usual confident self, making me momentarily wonder if I had imagined it all.

Entering the hallway, I immediately sensed an unusual stillness. Professor Hubertson's welcoming shout was missing and there was also no response when Jenny called aloud. 'Uncle, where are you?'

I silently prayed Professor Hubertson had not become unwell but not wanting to cause undue alarm began casually walking up to his study. 'He must be in his study, too engrossed to hear you.'

'OK. I'll organize dinner and you ask him to join us.'

Climbing up quickly I saw from the landing his half open door and him at his table, back towards me. He was very still and fearing the worst, my heart began to thump as I approached him slowly and said softly. 'Professor Hubertson?'

I was startled but instantaneously relieved when Professor Hubertson suddenly turned around and looked at me.

'Thank God, you are fine, Professor. For a moment I thought you weren't feeling good.'

For what seemed a very long time Professor Hubertson looked at me without a word. Then he slowly picked up a bundle of papers from the table and with a pained expression said, 'I didn't expect this from you.'

One look at my handwritten notes that he held told me everything; he now knew what I had hidden from him so long, that his project was a failure. I weakly tried to stutter an explanation, but Professor Hubertson merely gestured for me to sit. He looked shaken and I sat across him, fearful of what would follow, Jenny's wonderful news banished from my thoughts.

'Professor Hailey brought these papers today thinking I had mistakenly left them in the lab. Of course, I immediately knew they were yours, but having read a few lines could not stop. But first tell me how long have you known this?'

Just then Jenny came up and judging the somber situation stood quietly at the doorway. Seeing her Professor Hubertson said, 'Come dear. You should also sit in on this as it is very important.' Then, turning back to me he asked again, 'Yes, Rohan. You were about to tell me something.'

Not daring to look Professor Hubertson in the eye, I explained when and how exactly I had discovered the flaws, hastening to add that I was fearful how this would affect his health and so kept it secret.

Disbelief spread over Jenny's face and she spoke sharply. 'This is ridiculous. You are questioning Uncle and other top scientists in the world. I am sure you have made a terrible mistake.' Then, turning to her uncle she added kindly. 'I am indeed glad Rohan did not tell you as it would have caused you unnecessary concern. I am thankful he is so considerate.'

Stung by her quick assumption I was at fault, I retorted. 'But I am not wrong and he knows it!'

'Yes, dear. Rohan is not wrong,' replied Professor

Hubertson gravely. 'Indeed, I must thank him. I understand now why he did not inform me earlier, but I wish he had.'

I was bewildered; I had hidden my papers from the professor believing he wouldn't be able to withstand the setback yet here he was wishing I had told him earlier!

'Well, Rohan, let me first congratulate you on your observations. Indeed, the project cannot succeed in its present form. I am grateful you have opened my eyes to the fallacy of my assumptions, even though you had no intention to tell me.' Professor Hubertson chuckled, instantaneously releasing the tension. 'I am frankly astounded how I missed the errors we made. However, let me assure you the project shall not be wound up. Too many good men have laboured far too long for that.'

'But Professor,' I interrupted. 'Surely there is no way it can succeed! The proof is in your hands.'

'This proof only confirms that my work cannot be completed in the manner it is now being done.'

'What do you mean?'

'Your findings confirm what is wrong, but not what is right. I am convinced that despite your prognosis we will succeed if we revise our understanding and adopt a new strategy. This is no doubt a major setback, but it has only made me more determined than ever before to succeed.'

Though convinced otherwise, I knew better than to argue. Maybe a new approach, one I didn't know of, would work or he was deluding himself. In either case it seemed appropriate to ask, 'How much more time will it take?'

'I don't know right now. I propose to get my entire team together in a few days so you can present your findings to them. Then I will outline my new proposals. We will get a fix on the time frame once the initial analysis is done. I certainly don't expect it to be completed in a hurry.'

'Uncle, does it mean we would have to stay here till then,' asked Jenny.

'Yes, dear. Much as I wish to return to Sydney, I cannot do so till I complete my work. My entire life's work would be worth nothing if I were to fail in this most prestigious project entrusted to me by the Government.'

Again, the steely determination I had earlier noticed crept into Professor Hubertson's voice as he repeated. 'I cannot and will not fail those who depend upon me.'

'But, Uncle,' persisted Jenny. 'Can't you work in Sydney where the climate is much better for you?'

'I can, but you know the work is being done in Paris and here as well, and maximum progress has been made here. Of course, thanks to Rohan's brilliant work I now understand we were on the wrong track, but we can retrieve the project far more easily here.'

Perhaps realizing further argument was futile, Jenny kept quiet but I didn't like the implication of this decision. 'Professor Hubertson, can I ask you something?'

'Yes, of course, Rohan.'

'A new approach is akin to starting afresh and it's already been over three years. Would you really like Jenny to be here for a couple more years?'

'I never said that, did I? Jenny and you are free to take your own decisions.'

'I can't leave you alone when you are not even well!' Jenny despaired.

'I too want you with me, dear, but I cannot impose. You and Rohan are in love and I will be happy with whatever you decide. Of course, I would like it most if you both choose to be with me.'

'That can't be!' I burst out desperately. 'I have to go back home with Jenny.'

'As I just said, Rohan, I will be happy with whatever decision you both take.'

Seeing me losing patience, Jenny turned to me. 'Let us close the topic and have dinner. It has been a long day and I am sure everyone is as exhausted as I am.'

Dinner was a relatively quiet affair. Professor Hubertson was the only one keen to make conversation, asking a number of questions on my findings to which I replied in monosyllables for my thoughts were entirely on Jenny's pregnancy and its implications. In any case, I was convinced of the futility of his project.

Jenny too looked occupied, no doubt trying to cope with the difficult choices she faced. She obviously wished to be with her uncle in his old age and failing health, but also to settle down with me in view of her pregnancy. Her conflict was that my choice of settlement was not the same as her uncle's.

When she finally saw me off at the door, she leaned forward and whispered. 'I will speak to Uncle about what I told you in the park. I am sure he will take a decision in our interest.'

Early next morning I had a surprise visitor. I found Professor Hubertson in the living room chatting with Mrs Brown. This was only his second visit; the first when he had introduced me to Mrs Brown, having earlier negotiated with her for renting me a spare room.

'Good morning, Rohan,' he greeted warmly. 'I was passing by and thought you might be ready for breakfast and we could go home together. Shall we go if you are ready?'

'Good morning, Professor,' I replied. 'Yes, I was just leaving.'

It seemed odd why he would wish to accompany me

when I was just a few minutes away, but after walking for barely a hundred yards or so, Professor Hubertson stopped and turning to me said, 'I know you must have figured out that I especially came to see you. You see, I want to discuss something important and thought it better we do so without Jenny.'

'Sure, Professor. Please tell me.'

We walked on as he spoke in a measured tone. 'Jenny told me about her pregnancy last night. It was a complete shock. While I knew you two were drawn to each other, I had no idea it had gone so far. I admit I was at first angry, but since then I have thought over it calmly. You see, Rohan, Jenny is all I have and I would never allow her to be hurt. You also know I consider you my son. I am, therefore, happy that the two persons I love very much have decided to spend their lives together. The only problem is you wish to go to India while Jenny wants to be here with me. I tried to persuade her to accompany you, but she did not agree at all and wants to be with me to see the project succeed; maybe she realizes how much it means to me at the fag end of my life.'

Professor Hubertson paused and I suddenly realized how old and weighed down he looked. Time had indeed taken its toll and it saddened me.

'But Professor, are you really hopeful it will succeed?'

'I know you are convinced it won't, but after reading your notes all night I have identified the key issues requiring a fresh look. It will definitely be a success, but that is not important for now. Jenny's pregnancy has created a more critical situation.'

'Yes, I hope she will agree to accompany me to India where we can get married.'

'I am glad to hear that, but as I said before she is not ready to leave me alone despite my best attempts to convince her otherwise. On my part also I would not like to send her to an unknown place unless you are first married.'

'Then what do you suggest we do?'

'Now listen carefully, Rohan. I feel the best course is for you both to marry immediately and then leave for India. Then, you both return here and upon completion of the project we all leave together, me to Sydney and you both to wherever you wish to settle, India or Sydney. I made Jenny agree to this with great difficulty, assuring her nothing will happen to me in her brief absence.'

'But I can't marry without my parents even knowing!'

'You are to leave in a fortnight and Jenny can accompany you only if you get married. I am sure you will not want to leave her alone in her present condition. As I said, she is agreeable to this.'

The sun played hide-and-seek and it drizzled lightly. Jenny and I reached the office of the Registrar of Marriages, accompanied by Professor Hubertson and Mrs Brown. It was a short walk from home, but we took a cab since it was cold and Jenny insisted she would get married in her mother's wedding gown and refused to wear anything warm.

We sat quietly in a bare room before a stern official who laboriously entered our names in a thick, worn register. Having completed the task to his satisfaction, he filled in our names on a slip of paper and handed it to Professor Hubertson, recognizing him as the unquestioned leader of our pack, pointing him to another official at the far end.

This was the Registrar of Marriages who sat behind a huge desk on a raised platform in front of which were placed two rows of chairs. He was busy reading the day's newspaper and ignored us till Professor Hubertson coughed politely and wished him good morning. Then, grudgingly keeping aside the newspaper he stretched his hand for the slip of paper, at the same time gesturing us to sit.

After asking a few necessary questions he stood up, bade Jenny and I stand before him and proceeded to read out the marriage vows, asking us to repeat them after him, which we did in all sincerity. Then opening the Register of Marriages placed in front of him he entered the date '22 November 1925' and asked us to sign it followed by our witnesses, Professor Hubertson and Mrs Brown. With a flourish, the Registrar now pronounced us 'Man and Wife' and with that we were married.

Mrs Brown congratulated us warmly and Jenny started to cry a little when Professor Hubertson suddenly presented her with a bracelet, saying it was her mother's.

The formalities had taken less than ten minutes. Mrs Brown parted company to pick up groceries and Professor Hubertson left too, undoubtedly deeming it sensible to leave us newlyweds alone.

Jenny and I stood bewildered on the sidewalk in the busy market place with strangers pausing to look at us, me in my new suit and Jenny in her wedding gown. Acutely self-conscious and seeing Jenny unsure and fragile, I protectively held her only to find she was shivering uncontrollably. I quickly hailed a cab.

The most significant and overwhelming outcome our marriage brought about was that of Professor Hubertson formally escorting Jenny to my room that evening. As he said goodnight, Jenny suddenly rushed to him and, hugging him tight, cried her heart out. Professor Hubertson too became teary-eyed and watching them together made me realize the true meaning of the seemingly routine formality we had endured that morning. Jenny was leaving her home and she was my responsibility till death parted us.

Gently separating from Jenny, Professor Hubertson, powerless as only a father is when giving away his daughter, silently put her hand in mine and slowly walked away. With Jenny sobbing softly on my arm we watched him leave before silently going to my room—now her new home. It was a novel and beautiful experience knowing we would still be together in the morning.

As Jenny slept by my side, I lay awake deep into the night running my fingers softly through her hair but my thoughts were with Baoji and Ma. Feeling miserable for depriving them of the one pleasure every parent dreams of—-their child's marriage—-I prayed for forgiveness.

We left for India two days later, promising Professor Hubertson to return soon. On the long journey I often contemplated how dramatically my life had changed in only a few years; I had left home a young, unsure boy and was returning a married man about to be a father. I feared the mayhem this would cause, but the very next moment, visualizing how happy Baoji, Ma and Bhai would be to see me, I felt confident. Everything would be fine.

Ambala, Punjab: 1926

It seemed unbelievable but it was true. The long journey to Bombay was finally over, transporting me to a dramatically different environment. In an instant, the 'foreignness' I felt abroad vanished and amongst my own kind, savouring the sounds of my language and the smells of my dearly missed homeland, I felt a welcome anonymity steal over me. Not surprisingly, Jenny began feeling out of place and I held her reassuringly, as she nervously scanned the crowds.

Impatient to be with my family, the journey from Bombay to Ambala felt more excruciating than the longer sea journey earlier. On our way, I remembered how different my last train journey had been when I had left home, alone and sad. Now, I was returning with my love and feeling on top of the world.

The four-day train journey helped Jenny somewhat adjust to her new surroundings as she got accustomed to the crowds, languages, foods and grew much more relaxed by the time we rolled into Ambala station. But the familiar sights were now making *me* increasingly anxious. After a whispered discussion we agreed that to avoid shocking them, Jenny would stay back just a bit and I would meet my family first. We also decided to keep her pregnancy a secret.

Our train halted and we found ourselves in a cauldron of activities as *coolies* swarmed to collect baggage, passengers bargained portage, vendors shouted their wares and loud speakers announced the arrivals and departures. Jenny was becoming more anxious by the minute and my nervousness was turning into excitement. Even before I pulled out our bags from under our berths, I eagerly scanned the masses outside to spot my family.

The moment we stepped outside I saw Baoji and Bhai and instinctively rushed towards them shouting joyfully, 'Baoji, Bhai!' The next instant I was engulfed in Baoji's arms and the years slipped away as he wept and repeatedly kissed me, thanking God for bringing me home. And then Bhai hugged me tightly, crying tears of joy, and the warmth of their love transported me back to childhood.

A number of close relatives garlanded me and welcomed me with hugs and kisses. I spotted a child standing shyly behind Baoji and knew this could only be Saket, Bhai's son. Rushing forward I grabbed him and lifted him high in the air before catching him again as he burst out laughing. Only I knew how much I had missed my family!

Noticing Ma's absence, I asked, 'Where is Ma, Bhai?'

'She will welcome you at home. Let us go now, the tonga is waiting.'

At that moment I remembered Jenny! In my excitement I had completely forgotten about her and now, looking back, saw her standing at the same spot where I had left her, disoriented amidst the noisy multitude. Politely asking Baoji and Bhai to wait, I walked back to her.

When I returned with Jenny by my side, Baoji, Bhai and everyone else fell silent, watching us unsurely. And then, just as I had explained to her earlier, Jenny folded her hands, said 'Namaste' and touched Baoji's feet. Baoji looked at me perplexed and I explained, 'Baoji, this is Jenny, your daughter-in-law.'

Baoji was shocked and his face turned colourless. I knew

his singular thought was that his worst fear had come true, but he reflexively placed his hand upon Jenny's head to bless her. Bhai was equally shaken and extended his blessings silently and other relatives were no less stunned. Nobody spoke to Jenny and we silently trooped into our respective tongas.

The ride back home was strained, though I did my best to bring cheer by chatting with everybody and pointing out various places to Jenny. I felt bad for poor Jenny, who was obviously taken aback by the cold reception, but my greater fear was that this might change her mind about moving here permanently.

As we entered my neighbourhood, old memories came flooding back and I let them wash over me, enjoying glimpses of growing up, friends, school, and family. I sadly realized that one night, many years ago I had left my childhood here hoping to find it waiting on return, but time had passed on.

Even before the tonga stopped I saw Ma at the door, holding a plate peppered with small oil-lit earthen lamps to welcome me. As I rushed towards her, her eyes filled with tears. She silently stopped me from hugging her, bade me wait and began praying. Just then, she happened to look behind me and spotted Jenny. Her hands froze mid-air, her prayers stopped midway, and she looked questioningly, first at me and then at Baoji, who merely nodded.

For a moment Ma was at a loss and Jenny looked equally nonplussed. But then Ma seemed to make a visible effort and, leaving me standing, went forward and escorted Jenny upto the door, making her stand next to me before resuming her position on the other side of the door. She had prepared to welcome her son and was now ready for her daughter-in-law too.

Finishing her prayers, Ma put a vermilion tilak on our foreheads. She then kept her prayer plate aside and opened her arms to welcome us home and, holding me tight, cried out all the sadness she had bottled up these past years. Then she again hugged Jenny and with that one gesture accepted her into the family and dissolved my apprehensions.

Jenny's western clothes and her habit of calling me by my name initially caused considerable embarrassment to Baoji and Ma that compounded when an elder relative was present. The topic would then invariably turn to the ills of foreign rule. On account of the general misconception that westerners did not have stable marriages, they also had misgivings about how I had ruined my life by marrying Jenny. It did not help that Jenny's accent was largely beyond comprehension, though that mattered little to Ma and Bhabi since they didn't even know English. Thus, I became Jenny's official interpreter, but after some days I noticed no one needed me much.

Among those who we met first was my benefactor, Professor Hardayal, who had now retired. We respectfully touched his feet and gave him a few gifts and a letter Jenny carried from her uncle. Professor Hardayal was touched that I had not forgotten him and felt overjoyed to meet Jenny. It was an emotional moment for I now realized my debt to him for all my joyful experiences, including meeting Jenny. We talked for long about the Academy and Professor Hubertson and when we left I saw tears of joy in his eyes and felt redeemed.

All along, I had imagined living happily in Ambala with Jenny, but it was now clear that she was an outsider. Indeed, her very presence exaggerated things around her: garbage, stray animals, language, dresses people wore, street vendors, just about anything and everything. Sometimes I would stand aside to observe her in a crowd and wonder how her being foreign had never struck me earlier. For the first time, I began to wonder if it was fair to ask her to leave her world for mine.

Despite all problems, Jenny was obviously enjoying her stay. Baoji, Ma, and others were also comfortable with her now. It helped that she was now, at times, wearing a saree, having convinced Bhabi to teach her, and trying not to call me by my name in the presence of my parents. They were convinced that she would adjust and make this her home. But just when I thought things were going well, Jenny brought me back to reality. 'Rohan, these past two months have flown by fast. Your family is wonderful and I am really enjoying my stay, but my leave is ending. Moreover, I feel changes within me and must consult my doctor. It must also be hard for Uncle without me. We must head back home now.'

'Is everything alright? You can see a doctor here.'

'But you told me not to disclose my pregnancy, though I think Ma suspects.'

'Sure I did, but you saw how our marriage shocked everybody and it would have been worse to know you are pregnant. Also, then Ma and Baoji would insist their grandchild be born here.'

'No way that will ever happen, Rohan.'

'Why, what is wrong with that?'

'Don't forget I don't speak the language, nobody understands me, and from what I have seen so far I can well imagine the miserable condition of hospitals. I refuse to even consider it.'

Jenny was getting anxious and fearing that her voice would

carry outside our room, I quickly gestured her to calm down and spoke gently. 'Dear, please relax. I am equally concerned about our baby and I see your point. I had also promised Professor Hubertson to return soon. I just hope that having met my family you are comfortable about settling here once your uncle's work is done.'

Jenny tenderly rested her head upon my chest. 'I am sorry, Rohan. I am getting cranky nowadays, maybe because of the baby. I promise I will seriously consider coming here after Uncle moves to Sydney. You know I have no real interest in Glendale, but right now it frightens me to be having a baby and I feel reassured about the facilities there.'

'Of course, everything will be fine. Don't worry.'

Next morning, while we were all having tea and Jenny was in her room I informed Ma I had to return whereupon she quietly picked up the empty teacups and unhappily went to the kitchen. But Baoji reacted impatiently. 'What do you mean you are returning? You have hardly been here. I thought you had come back to support us in our old age.'

'Baoji, I will definitely do that but we have to first wind up there. The project would take another six months and we will be back then.'

'Are you sure Jenny will agree?'

'Of course, she will. You can see she is very happy here.'

I could see Baoji losing his temper as he continued. 'I am not too sure. The elders were right when they told me that sending your son abroad is to lose him forever. I hoped you were different, but you married a foreigner and will now never come back. You have spoiled your life and will regret this when you are old. Living abroad, far from us, you will one day learn your Baoji and Ma are no more and will not even be able to see us one last time.'

Just then, looking more in control, Ma entered and scolded

Baoji. 'What is this you keep saying? I know my son well and if he says he will be back, he will. Now stop this discussion immediately. What impression will Jenny carry if she hears you?'

Baoji became quiet and I too sat quietly not sure how to react. After some time, Bhai spoke gently. 'Rohan, the western world provides material comforts, but it can never be your real home where you enjoy your own language, food or the company of your people. Once children are born you will be compelled to stay on for their sake, but one day they will go their way and you will be alone, neither belonging there nor here. I am told most elders live in old age homes abroad and their children do not even visit them, but in our culture a family member never leaves your side. Jenny is a wonderful girl who will adjust very well here and I believe you owe it to yourself, if not to Baoji and Ma, to come back.'

'Of course, Bhai, I just said we would return soon. There is no question of not doing so. I just need some more time.'

'I believe you, son,' said Ma. 'We want you to be happy wherever you are but we believe your real happiness lies here in your own land. Let us now change the topic and enjoy the few days we have together. That reminds me, I want to ask you and Jenny something.'

'What is it, Ma?'

'Baoji and I have discussed this. Call us old fashioned if you like, but we find it difficult to accept your court marriage. So, this Sunday I will call a pandit for a proper wedding. I am confident Jenny will agree and if you can't ask her I will. We planned for your wedding each day you were away and I hope you won't deprive us this joy.'

As she spoke, Ma began to get emotional while Baoji sat quietly but still visibly disturbed. Unsure how Jenny would react I didn't know what to say. Just then, she walked in and sensing something amiss put a consoling hand on Ma's shoulder before turning to me. 'What happened? Why is Ma crying?'

'Nothing, Jenny. You should go to your room.'

'No. I want to know what happened. Bhai, can you not tell me, please?'

'She is disturbed about your return. Also, she wishes to organize a marriage ceremony for you and Rohan before you leave.'

'Why, that is wonderful!' Jenny exclaimed in delight. 'I have heard so much of weddings here and would love to dress up as an Indian bride.' Then turning to Ma she said, 'You know, I lost Mom at an early age and nothing would please me more than for you to treat me as your daughter and for Baoji to give me away in marriage.'

Jenny's enthusiasm transformed the atmosphere and Ma and Baoji happily got busy planning the wedding. Instead of the traditional elaborate affair they decided on a simple ceremony with only immediate family members present. Professor Hardayal was a special invitee.

Despite its simplicity, the excitement of the wedding was palpable. Baoji was his usual self, supervising arrangements and ordering everyone about in various tasks. Bhai took leave from office to attend to various formalities and Ma, Bhabi and Jenny got busy shopping.

An unanticipated fallout was that, for undisclosed reasons, Ma forbade Jenny and me from sleeping in the same room so, she moved in with Bhabi and I with Bhai. Of course, we were together all day but at night we would retire to our separate rooms. Jenny loved the pretense and played the part of a bride-to-be to perfection. These were fun-filled times, especially for the children who found it unique to participate in a marriage of an already married couple.

Lying awake at night, watching Bhai sleeping soundly by my side, my thoughts would invariably go back to the time we shared this room. So much had happened in between, but at that moment it appeared time had stood still all this while. And that felt good.

It was soon Sunday and as I got ready the house began to fill up with guests; traditionally weddings took place in the evening, but for the sake of convenience ours was in the morning. In another part of the house Jenny got ready, which included being adorned with beautiful designs of mehendi, as people around sang songs. Usually the bridegroom arrived at the bride's house on horseback with a procession of relatives and friends, but I quietly came out of my room and sat beside Pandit Hari Ram Shankar, who had since arrived and lit the holy fire.

Soon, Pandit Hari Ram Shankar announced the auspicious time was upon us, and Ma and Bhabi ceremoniously escorted Jenny. She wore a traditional red saree as her face hid from view behind a veil. I stood up to formally exchange marigold garlands with her and then we both sat cross-legged on the floor. The pandit began chanting shlokas invoking blessings of Agni, God of Fire. We sat for a long time, feeding the fire with ghee from time to time, as directed, with legs cramping and eyes stinging from the thick smoke blowing directly into our eyes. Finally, when I was about to give up in pain, he asked us to stand. As he read from the scriptures, we walked seven times around the holy fire, a cloth held by me tied to Jenny's saree. Then, as everyone loudly cheered and showered flowers on us, Pandit Hari Ram Shankar pronounced us 'Husband and Wife'.

Jenny and I touched Baoji and Ma's feet to seek blessings and as they emotionally hugged us tight, I saw Jenny too was moved. Pandit Hari Ram Shankar took his offering and went away after blessing us once more and we sat down for a feast.

It was late afternoon when the last guest left and looking at Baoji and Ma, I realized how much this meant to them. Personally, the most important outcome of the ceremony was that evening Jenny was allowed to return to my room.

Jenny's cheerful participation dispelled their fears and assured Baoji and Ma of my return. Thankfully, nobody spoke directly to her on the subject though Ma tried to probe, but partly due to the language barrier and partly due to my timely interventions she did not succeed. Once I overheard Baoji and Ma talk about how Jenny was better than the modern Indian girls they heard of and it pleased me immensely. They were now so impressed with her that it seemed it would be my fault and not hers if we were not to settle down with them! In any case, my departure was far less emotional for they believed we would very soon return permanently. As did I.

Glendale, Ontario: 1926–1934

Our daughter Riya was born on 17 July 1926. It was not an easy pregnancy for Jenny and it did not help that both Professor Hubertson and I were completely at sea. I wished often we were home with Ma, but she was far away. When told, Ma had, of course, immediately realized we had hidden this during our stay with her and was upset. Bhai sent me a long letter stating that had she known Ma would never have let us go. But she was a mother and could not remain angry for long.

The frequency of Bhai's letters increased as Ma counseled us through the pregnancy. Applying the wisdom imbibed from her mother and her own experiences, she detailed various precautions that Bhai dutifully conveyed. Her sermons covered every possible aspect, but laid particular stress on two critical elements: the first, Jenny's diet and the second, the prayers she must offer. Though Baoji and Ma never said it, I suspected that their recommended diet and prayers were aimed at the birth of a male grandchild.

Ma's sincere suggestions ironically caused much merriment. On my insistence Jenny discussed the diet with her doctor who brushed it aside and that was that. As for the prayers, my translation of these from Urdu into English made their reading hilarious. It was obvious Jenny would never chant them and, thinking of poor Ma, I began doing so instead until I discovered that they were meant only for the expectant mother!

The expected day drew nearer and our anxiety increased considerably. Jenny was high strung and completely emotionally dependent upon me so I stopped going to work. Professor Hubertson was excited beyond words as he awaited the addition to his family and back home in India, Ma arranged special prayers for the safe delivery of the baby.

That early morning, when Professor Hubertson and I rushed Jenny to the hospital, I felt overwhelmed. The doctor was ahead of her time and allowed me to stand in a sterile green gown behind Jenny, who writhed in agony, screaming for God to save her in the delivery room.

As the interval between contractions reduced and the pain increased beyond bearing, the doctor ordered Jenny to push, which she did with strength I could not imagine. Finally, her entire face covered with perspiration, I saw her make one great effort before giving up and almost fainting. I desperately rushed to her side when the doctor called out, 'Well done. You have done it.' I looked up to see the doctor bent between Jenny's legs and a few seconds later straighten, holding a tiny baby. 'Congratulations, it's a girl.'

As I kissed her brow, Jenny opened her eyes and smiled weakly, giving me a slight, exhausted squeeze just when the doctor who was cleaning the baby looked at me. 'You look like you're about to faint! Better sit and have some water.'

Her work done, the doctor placed our child next to Jenny and I leaned forward for a glimpse. She was tinier than I could have ever imagined a human child to be yet she had a perfectly chiseled nose, eyes, ears, lips and soft light blonde hair on her head. As I looked upon her angelic face, she opened her eyes just a little and in them I saw my own reflection. I turned to Jenny and softly kissed her on her forehead. 'Thank you.'

Explaining they would monitor the baby for a few hours, the doctor took her away while Jenny, already asleep, was wheeled to her room.

Just as I stepped out, I met Professor Hubertson who jumped with joy on hearing the news and excitedly rushed towards the nursery. 'I cannot wait anymore to see the baby. Go telegram the good news to your family.' At that moment I truly realized we were a family.

Rushing to a nearby post office, I shot off a telegram to Baoji, choosing the words carefully: 'Your granddaughter, Riya, born today at 1:46:10 pm. Mother and child well. Congratulations!' It was important to mention the exact time for I knew Baoji would need it to make the baby's birth chart—a must back home.

Walking back, I couldn't help but feel a little sad that Baoji and Ma would hear of this addition to their family only after some days. I knew their initial reaction would be subdued on finding out that it is a baby girl and I could almost see Ma blame this on me for not following her directions faithfully. Then I smiled upon visualizing Baoji rereading the telegram and pointing out the name of the child to Ma—Riya—which would immediately mollify her. They would then gather neighbours and relatives, distribute sweets and have a prayer to thank God for his blessings. Such was the tradition back home. As I bought fresh flowers for Jenny, I quietly thanked her for agreeing to name our daughter after my grandmother.

It was truly amazing how a tiny child sleeping innocently all day in one small corner of a bed could fill up an entire household with her presence. Her arrival bonded Jenny and me in a hitherto undiscovered intimate way we could not have imagined. Yet I observed the most dramatic change in Professor Hubertson.

Due to practical considerations, Jenny and I now lived with the Professor. He began getting up early each morning, while Jenny and I slept, to pick Riya from her crib and spend hours playing with her. He grudgingly left for work only to rush back at the earliest opportunity to be with her. Riya's arrival seemed to breathe fresh life into him and he looked as if he'd turned younger overnight. I had never seen him so happy before.

Riya began growing and her antics made each day exciting and joyful for us. When she was four months old, Jenny rejoined work and it fell upon Professor Hubertson and me to take care of the baby. I had already lost interest in the project, but continued working on it since I had no alternative. I offered to work part-time, but Professor Hubertson felt that since I was a junior it would set a bad precedent. His own position was different and he gladly volunteered to work from home to look after Riya. Jenny's library was nearby so she could come home for lunch and spend some time with Riya too. Thus, between the two of them, someone was always there with Riya and it became common for me to daily receive a number of calls from Professor Hubertson, excitedly detailing each of her wonderful actions. When I came back from work he would reluctantly hand her over to me.

It always brought a smile to my face whenever Professor Hubertson held Riya and commented how much she looked like Jenny's mom; I was convinced she resembled Ma. Often Professor Hubertson would doze in his armchair with Riya sleeping soundly in his arms and Jenny would whisper, 'Dear, look at him. I am so glad to see Uncle happy and it is all thanks to our bundle of joy.'

I too was happy yet something had begun to gnaw deep inside, which I was unable to pin down. Then, one day when I was watching Jenny nurse the child she said, 'Riya's arrival is a tonic for Uncle,' and suddenly it dawned on me what was bothering me. It obviously showed, for Jenny immediately asked, 'What's the matter, Rohan? Are you OK?'

Taking a deep breath, I chose my words carefully. 'Something has been bothering me lately and looking at Riya just now made me realize what it is. You remember when she was born how frequently I sent photographs of her to Baoji and Ma? Maybe that was my feeble endeavor to include them in my life and imagining them happy served as a balm. However, Riya is growing up quickly and I feel sad that Baoji and Ma have not even seen her, let alone hold and play with her. They are missing out on the joy of watching her grow and it's somehow making me feel that I too am moving further away from them.'

Jenny was quiet for some time and then carefully placing Riya on the bed she walked over to me and cupping my face in her hands said softly. 'It is indeed sad Baoji and Ma are so far away, but just a few days back Uncle told me that his work will be done shortly and then we will return home. On the way we will stay with them for some time.'

'Have you forgotten what I told you?' I retorted angrily. 'Mark my words: the project is doomed to fail. Your uncle is deluding himself, he will never complete the project or return to Sydney.'

Stunned by my sudden outburst, Jenny quietly retreated and I rushed to her apologizing. 'Oh Jenny, I am so sorry. I didn't mean to shout.'

'Don't worry, I understand.'

'It's just that Baoji and Ma are getting on in age and time is slipping away. Don't you think I owe it to them to be with them?'

'Of course, I do. But Riya is so small if we take her now the heat and mosquitoes will make her ill. So be patient and we will go when she becomes a bit older and stronger. I am sure by then Uncle's work will also be over.'

'I assure you Riya will be absolutely fine in India. I too was born there and here I am standing before you. Also, it is my dearest wish the Professor succeeds but I know better. Anyway, let us target our departure for six months from now. If Professor Hubertson is correct, his work will be done by then and Riya will also be stronger. I suggest you discuss this with him and I will write to Baoji informing him we shall be home for Riya's first birthday.'

'OK dear. This sounds good. Now let us go to sleep.'

'I shall also begin looking for a job back home.'

'But would it not be far easier to get one in Sydney?'

'Sure, I could look at that too, but I want to try India first. I want my child to know her roots.'

'Yes, that is important, but you know something, we humans are so adaptable that I feel Glendale is my home now.'

'And that is exactly why I am confident you will love Ambala too.'

'*Touché*! Good night, dear.'

Giving me a lovely smile Jenny switched off the lamp and we both drifted off to sleep.

I never did get to write the letter to Baoji to inform him of our arrival, which would only have raised his hopes to be disappointed yet again. I was at work when Jenny gave me a ring.

'Rohan, I hope you are not too busy right now?'

'Not at all, in fact I myself wanted to call you. You remember Professor Bill Hayes, who we met the other day with Sana?'

'Of course, I do. I like them and we must get them over for drinks.'

'Yes, but listen, I mentioned to Bill about moving to India and he told me his company is opening a lab there and with my experience I stand a good chance of getting in. Will it not be great if it works out?'

'Yes, that is good news. But did you also find out about any openings in Sydney?'

'But that will not be necessary if I get a job in India.'

'There is no harm in keeping one's options open, is there?'

'OK, I will find out about that too. By the way what did you want to tell me?'

'Oh! I almost forgot. Well, I spoke to Uncle and he fully understands your keenness to be with your family, but his assessment is that currently your specialization may not be in much demand in India. He promised to ask around and let us know of the opportunities.'

'I am happy to know that he is fine with us going back, but I just told you what Bill said. Anyway, what did he say about his return to Sydney?'

'I was coming to that. He believes his work will take around ten months and he wondered if we could wait till then so we can travel together. He would like to spend some time in India sightseeing and visiting his friend, your old professor...what's his name?'

'Professor Hardayal. But Jenny, what about my plan to celebrate Riya's first birthday at home?'

'Be reasonable, Rohan. This is such a small request from Uncle. I think we should agree. After all, we can always celebrate her other birthdays with your parents.'

'Let me think it over. But tell me, dear, are you fine living in India with me?'

There was a long pause after which Jenny replied, 'I will be honest. I am not completely sure I can adjust. I can never forget how uncomfortable it was with everybody staring at me wherever I went. But I am willing to try for your happiness.'

'Thank you, Jenny. You have made me very happy. Trust me you will love it there. I guess we can agree to Professor Hubertson's suggestion, but I insist we go back after ten months even if his work is not complete. Is that OK?'

'Alright, we can finalize this in the evening.'

That evening we debated various alternatives. Jenny seemed most comfortable with the status quo, making me realize for the first time her attachment to Glendale because our daughter was born here. Of course, she was also enjoying her job and had good friends. Professor Hubertson was pragmatic about his health not permitting him to work for long and he was prepared to settle in Sydney. I was clear I had to return to Baoji, Ma and Bhai.

All this while, as we discussed options, Riya played in Professor Hubertson's lap and I began to realize how truly alone he was in the world. We were his family and I knew he would find it impossible to be parted from Jenny and Riya. I was also frightened how he would handle the disappointment when his project failed. I owed him much and wished there was some common ground.

After a lengthy discussion, we all decided to leave for India after exactly ten months; Professor Hubertson was supremely confident of wrapping up his work by then. He would then go onwards to Sydney, leaving us behind to decide where to settle. We promised to visit him every six months in case we chose India. Relieved something concrete had finally shaped up, I asked Jenny, 'Are you happy?'

'Of course, I am. It will be great to show Riya your birthplace then mine, she will be so excited to see where we first met!'

'Yes, that will be great. I have so many happy memories of Sydney.'

'But one day I would also like to bring her back here to see where she was born.'

'We will do that too.'

The course was charted and I wrote home to inform them of our plans and got a prompt and jubilant reply. Bhai wrote that Baoji planned to get the house completely renovated and went about telling everybody that nothing but the best would do for his for his foreign-born daughter-in-law and granddaughter. We would reach around Diwali, a joyous festival of lights celebrating the homecoming of Lord Rama after fourteen long years, and Ma compared my return to that.

Life became hectic overnight as I got busy exploring various job options and winding up my affairs. At times it appeared Professor Hubertson was correct there were few jobs back home, but nothing disheartened me. The very thought of being home was uplifting, though I knew Glendale would always be special as the place where I married Jenny and where Riya was born.

Everything was going according to plan and I was ready to book our return passage. But each time I asked Professor Hubertson for a firm date, he changed the topic. This initially caused me misgivings, but then seeing him work feverishly I felt ashamed for doubting him. I finally spoke to Jenny. 'The agent says we must book now or the fares will go up considerably, but your uncle is not giving me a date. Can you not ask him?'

'I was just going to tell you that at lunch I discussed it with him. He had something to say and I told him we should talk it over with you.'

'What did he say?'

'Well, he says he needs another two to three months. He was being a dear suggesting we go ahead of him on schedule and he will follow, but I offered to postpone our departure so we can go together. I hope that is fine with you?'

Suddenly losing temper I shouted, 'NO! That is not fine with me. How can you promise without asking me? I have already informed Baoji and they are making big plans. How can I disappoint them? I know the project will never get done so we must leave as planned and if need be, without him.'

For the next few minutes I angrily rambled on about how unfair Professor Hubertson and she were to go back on their word while she looked at me silently without reacting. Finally, my anger spent, I sat down silently and Jenny replied calmly. 'Don't be upset. Uncle has nothing to do with this, I told you he said we should not change our program. It was I who thought we should not leave him alone in view of his health and because he will miss Riya dearly. I also felt a few months here or there should not matter much. Anyway, it is your call and I will agree to whatever you decide. But just bear in mind that we will not be able to forgive ourselves if, God forbid, something happens to Uncle while he is alone here.'

I knew in my heart what Jenny said made sense. There was another factor: that same morning Bill had informed me that the opening of the laboratory had been deferred. This meant there was no job for me at home. Moreover, a few hours back, Kingston University had offered me a wonderful teaching assignment, but that required a one-year commitment. I silently reached into my coat pocket and handed Jenny the appointment letter.

'This is wonderful, Rohan!' Jenny exclaimed reading it. 'This is exactly your subject of interest and they are offering a handsome salary.' Then she sobered and added, 'But this is not important if you want to go home.'

'Bill told me his project will take time and I have not found any other job so far. That means if we go back as planned I will be without a job.'

'Could you not work at the university till the lab opens, and we can go back with Uncle?'

'I could work for a year, by then the lab will surely be ready and Professor Hubertson will also be free. This assignment will give us sufficient money so even if something unforeseen happens we will be comfortable. What do you think?'

'It is fine with me if you are OK with it.'

'It makes sense. I will write to Baoji tomorrow and I am sure he will understand. Since we are moving permanently to India, a few more months here will make no difference. You can convey this to your uncle too.'

Bhai wrote that Baoji and Ma celebrated Diwali in a somber mood. At first, Baoji lost his temper and shouted that I would never return. He then withdrew into a shell and simply refused to discuss the matter. Ma had taken my side and tried to explain to him that I too must be unhappy about the change of plan and I would surely return soon. However, Bhai later overheard her pray for my early return in the privacy of her kitchen temple; I guess while putting up a brave front she was trying to overcome her own fear. Bhai's own acute disappointment was also evident, though I knew he would never say it directly.

Bhai's words had me wishing I could somehow go back right away, but it was too late for I had committed to the university and Jenny had also informed her supervisor that she was staying on. I resolved there would be no more changes and I would return home immediately once my contract was over.

Teaching engaged me full time. I enjoyed the work and it was good money, but each weekend I faithfully reviewed my applications to the various institutions in India. Unfortunately, I either got no reply or the offer paled in comparison to my present job. I was, of course, prepared for a salary cut, but didn't want to compromise on job satisfaction and the few offers I received were not of interest. I was banking on Bill's project, but to my great disappointment that got shelved. The days slipped into months and soon one year was over, but I was no closer to returning home. It did not help that the university offered a new contract at enhanced my salary.

Professor Hubertson kept busy but as I had predicted, his work was no nearer to completion. I could not understand how, despite lack of results and the government tightening its purse strings due to recession, his work continued to get funding but it did and the good professor continued to toil.

During this time Jenny got promoted and took on greater responsibility and since Professor Hubertson was spending more time at work we hired Mrs Brown, my old landlady, as a full-time babysitter for Riya.

My inability to firm up my departure date had an unanticipated fall out. Letters from home no longer contained the almost mandatory impassioned plea from Baoji and Ma for me to return. This made me sad, though I knew they were merely giving me freedom to decide. I had no doubt my future was in Ambala, but with each passing day I was losing control of the situation, especially as Jenny no longer spoke of moving, even to Sydney. I knew I had to do something, and fast.

'Rohan, when you are back I would like to show you the results of some tests we are currently running,' called out Professor Hubertson, as I was leaving for work.

'Of course, Professor.'

'Riya and I are now going to the park so she can play on the new slides.'

Just then Riya came running into the Professor's arms and I smiled, as she waved to me, 'Bye, D.' She was growing up wonderfully, charming everyone with her non-stop prattle and I had begun teaching her Hindi and tried to make her call me 'Baoji,' just like Bhai and I called our father, but she preferred 'D', short for Daddy. In looks she was clearly my daughter, but in speech she was like any Canadian.

Driving to work, I mulled over Professor Hubertson's words, finding his invitation unusual since he had stopped discussing his work with me for some time now.

My curiosity was aroused and all day I kept wondering if Professor Hubertson had indeed somehow made a breakthrough. Realizing this could translate into our return home, I waited anxiously for the day's work to be over. Finally, after what seemed unbearably long, my lectures got completed and I proceeded to the parking lot.

Just as I stepped out of the administrative block I heard a call from behind. 'Mr Rohan. Please wait.' It was Miranda from the reception gesturing towards the telephone receiver she held out for me. I retraced my steps. 'Who is it?'

'It's a Mrs Brown. She says it is urgent.'

Fearing Riya had hurt herself I hurriedly took the phone. 'Hello, Mrs Brown. What is it? Is Riya fine?'

'She is fine, but I am afraid I have bad news. Professor Hubertson felt unwell and Jenny has taken him to the hospital. She asked me to call you and wants you to reach there immediately.'

'Thanks, Mrs Brown. I am going there now. Please be with Riya till we return.'

Fearing the worst I drove fast to the hospital and ran inside to see Jenny near the reception. She seemed stiff as a stone, looking right at me. When I came closer she whispered, 'You are too late,' before silently swooning in my arms.

Hundreds attended Professor Hubertson's burial, including dignitaries from the Australian High Commission, European Academy of Science and the Australian Academy of Sciences. Top scientists recalled their long association with him and described his passing as a blow to the world of science. Neighbours placed wreaths on his grave and recounted memories of their distinguished neighbor in the presence of international media.

Jenny, who had few memories of her real father and had now lost the only father figure she had known, bore her loss stoically. It was heartbreaking to see little Riya ask when her Grandpa would be back. My only consolation was not moving to India as once planned, and making Professor Hubertson's last days happy with Jenny and Riya.

Jenny told me that on that fateful day she had come home for lunch and found Professor Hubertson sleeping on his armchair with Riya asleep in his arms. They both looked so peaceful and contended that she quietly took their photograph before carefully picking up Riya and placing her on her bed. She then picked up a light blanket to cover her uncle and noticed his erratic breathing. When he did not respond to her frantic attempts to wake him, she immediately called an ambulance. She said she would never forget that on the way to the hospital her uncle had briefly looked at her, and softly pressed her hand to comfort her. That was the last time he opened his eyes.

I wondered for long what Professor Hubertson wanted to show me that particular evening and even went through his papers, but I had been away from the project far too long to catch up with the developments. Anyway, knowing it would not succeed, I felt relieved the good soul was saved the disappointment. I turned over his papers to Bill, who succeeded as project leader.

It was exactly six months later that Jenny and I were special invitees for the unveiling of Professor Hubertson's portrait in his lab's library to mark the successful conclusion of his project. He had been correct all along and I was happy he had proved me completely wrong.

Patents from Professor Hubertson's revolutionary discoveries in chemical bonds eventually earned millions. As arranged by him, this led to the establishment of endowments for deserving students at the Science Academies at Paris, Sydney and Ottawa. A lump formed in my throat when I learned he had especially instituted a handsome scholarship for Indian students for undergraduate studies at the Australian Academy of Sciences. For a long time, I wished I could somehow retrace my steps in time and seek forgiveness for doubting him.

Life became routine again as Riya got busy at school and Jenny seemed to overcome her grief. However, Professor Hubertson's death made me increasingly reflect on Baoji and Ma. I began to dread receiving bad news about them, often waking up with cold sweats in middle of the night. Once again, I began to plan on going home; with her uncle's demise, Jenny was no longer keen to return to Sydney and instead arranged to dispose his house. I reasoned with her that we had a choice, either here, in Glendale, or Ambala and since we had no family here the latter made sense. After a long debate Jenny left the decision up to to me, but a few days later became pregnant with our second child.

Sanjay was born on 8 February 1930 and Bhai replied to my telegram saying that Baoji and Ma had a grand celebration, thanking God for blessing us with a son to carry forward my name even if, as Baoji put it, in another world. He also cautioned that once children grew up, it would be impossible for me to return so it had to be either now or never.

In so many small ways I saw for myself we had begun to grow roots in Glendale, enjoying a slow-paced comfortable life insulated from misfortune commonplace in big cities wrecked by what later came to be called the Great Depression. So, once again I renewed my efforts to convince Jenny to move to Ambala, happy when she finally agreed to visit there to explore the possibility. But then we had to wait for little Sanjay to grow up so he could withstand the strenuous journey and since Riya had begun school, we had to take her vacations into account. It was only when Sanjay was almost five years old that I found myself headed towards the land of my birth.

Ambala, Punjab: 1934

The summer of 1934 was when I first comprehended I might never return home permanently, but for some unfathomable reason I refused to accept this for years thereafter.

Determined to spend each minute capturing my days of youth and familiarize Jenny with the Indian way of life, we visited various places, even traveling as far as to Chandni Chowk in Old Delhi and Lutyens in New Delhi; the harmonious co-existence of ancient traditions and modern life had Jenny wonderstruck. As we walked the streets, Bhai and I relived our childhood, remembering old friends and the joys of growing up. Lachhu Pahelwan, Bhai told me, had left the army to join the freedom movement and had participated in Gandhiji's Dandi March two years back. Our childhood friends were by and large leading decent lower-middle class lives, accepting life's struggles with equanimity. It was amazing how, in comparison, we both had travelled far and wide and enjoyed success that seemed impossible at one time. Life had been too kind and we had Baoji and Ma to thank for sacrificing everything for us.

Despite difficulties with Hindi, though they understood a few words, Riya and Sanjay were having a whale of a time, thrilled to be in a wonderland of crowds, noise, laughter, and delicious food. Particularly fascinated by all sorts of animals freely moving about in streets, we would take numerous photographs each time they came across an elephant, cow, goat or monkey. There was never a dull moment and if nothing else, Bhai's children would take them around the neighbourhood. Everybody treated them like royalty because of the sheer novelty of them being foreigners, albeit with an Indian father. Ma cooked for them all day and, despite Jenny's concerns about unboiled water and spicy food, they relished each meal. This particularly pleased Baoji and Ma who boasted that their grandchildren were completely Indian.

It was obvious that while the children had more comforts in Glendale they certainly got more love here. Riya seemed to have replaced Professor Hubertson with Baoji while Sanjay's favorite was Ma and he would follow her all over, eating from her hand. It was a joy to watch Baoji and Ma laugh and discuss their antics all day and I could not have asked God for anything more.

All this while, anxious to obtain Jenny's consent, I did everything I could to ensure her comfort. The house was overcrowded, but we had our own bedroom while the children slept with Baoji and Ma. I got window screens to keep out mosquitoes and flies, and personally tried getting rid of lizards. I also bought air coolers which made it possible to sleep during hot nights, though once the children had slept Baoji often switched the one in his room off in order to save on electricity. His philosophy was that if he and his children had grown up without such comforts there was no need to pamper the grandchildren.

To everyone's amusement, I got an English commode installed. Though this was Jenny's second visit and she was familiar with the Indian toilet requiring a person to squat, she found it miserable. The new commode brought her immense relief and also became the envy of the neighbourhood when

Baoji began bringing over friends to show them the new contraption.

Outside our house, Jenny showed tremendous fortitude despite everyone gawking at her and beggars expecting a windfall on the account that she was white. Particularly disturbing to her were the large crowds and loud noises in every market and street, which made her fear a riot would break out any moment or she was already in midst of one. She eventually adjusted but remained wary, always firmly holding onto little Sanjay and Riya. What she could not really adjust to was the abject poverty she saw everywhere. Often we would be savouring tasty dishes at a restaurant, but Jenny could not bring herself to eat. She would quietly pack her food and give it to beggars looking in through the window. I guessed that having grown up here, Bhai and I were immune to this dismal reality, but Jenny's own world was less real in this respect.

Whenever we visited friends or relatives, a feast would be prepared for us. Jenny would gamely try new dishes, politely inquiring about their preparation but this invariably led to more of the same stuff being piled on her plate. She struggled to figure out a way to be polite yet escape a second or third helping.

Frequent power outages were another problem as they often left us perspiring heavily. Jenny initially found a solution by taking long baths and stepping out only when power was restored. However, when her long baths began adding to our water shortage problems, she began braving the uncomfortable heat without complaint.

One day Bhai considerately invested in a diesel generator that became the envy of the neighbourhood. I excitedly waited for power cuts and rushed to crank the generator and bask in its glory. Unfortunately, it took ten minutes of hard labour to start, resulting in achy arms for the next few days. The unbearable racket it generated was seemingly equal to a hundred railway locomotives and like them spewed sooty noxious fumes. We had to choose between darkness and heat on the one hand and unbearable noise and smoke on the other. The majority vote, gleefully endorsed by the entire neighbourhood, was for the former.

Jenny shared her experiences in the privacy of our bedroom, marveling at the historical and cultural richness she saw but acutely disturbed by the public spectacle of poverty, disease and hunger. One evening, as we lay to sleep she asked, 'Rohan, you and Bhai laugh together all the time and I see the love in your family and understand you must miss them so much when abroad, but do you really miss the stark poverty, the filth...?'

She was looking at me with such innocent curiosity that I burst out laughing. 'C'mon dear, nobody likes grimy streets, harsh summer heat, thirst, hunger and disease. But these are part of life here and we are conditioned to accept them. In fact, I notice it much more now than I did before.'

'One can condition oneself to undesirable things, but certainly no one can *miss* such a life.'

'Frankly, Jenny, I miss my family and way of life. There is so much beauty and joy in the vibrant colors, different smells, delicious foods, and boisterous crowds. Each sound in the streets, whether it is the laugh of a half-naked child running after a falling kite or a mango-seller calling customers or even the perhaps distasteful cry of a beggar for alms, makes life so real and joyful.'

'But then why don't I see people happy? Even when you and Bhai laugh publicly bystanders look strangely at you.'

'Let's sleep, dear. I am tired.'

Jenny did not press for a reply, but I mulled her question long after she had dozed off. As sleep enveloped me, I knew I had not convinced her why I loved my birthplace and wished she simply accepted the fact that I belonged here.

One evening, Jenny, Bhabi and the children were attending someone's engagement ceremony. Jenny was curious upon learning that it was an arranged marriage and the couple would be meeting for the first time. I was in my room when Ma called. 'Rohan, come for tea. It is getting cold.'

Baoji and Bhai were already in the living room and Ma served tea. After finishing his tea, Baoji kept his cup aside and asked, 'Son, have you decided?'

'About what, Baoji?'

The matter had obviously already been discussed in my absence and Bhai explained. 'About you coming back.'

'Of course, I shall come back for good.'

Ma could not stop herself and chided. 'When you first went overseas you said you will be back after studies, but did not. After that you said you will work for one year and come back, but again you did not. Not only that, you married a foreigner without telling us. If you don't intend to return, why don't you say so once and for all?'

Baoji intervened. 'Rohan, we have seen more life than you. We only wish you happiness and the longer you live abroad, especially now that you have children, the more difficult it will be to return. It is our duty to guide you and tell you that living abroad is fine when you are young, but you will regret it when you get older. For your happiness we want you here among your own people and family. This will comfort us too.' Then, turning to Bhai he added. 'Why don't you say something too?'

Bhai spoke hesitatingly and I could see he was being careful to not upset me. 'Rohan, you will get a fine job here and though Jenny may initially find it difficult she will adjust just as you did abroad. There are so many foreigners living here permanently.'

Taken aback by the bluntness of the conversation, I mumbled. 'I have no plans to settle abroad, but let me first discuss this with Jenny.'

Baoji retorted impatiently. 'If you are clear about settling here then where is the need to ask Jenny? She is your wife. She will do as you say.'

'No, Baoji. I must know her views before I take a decision. It will mean asking her to make a sacrifice.'

'Since when has a woman living with her husband in his land been a sacrifice?'

'I did not mean that. I only meant that I must know her mind at least.'

'Have you not spoken to her at all or were you lying before?'

Baoji was losing his temper and Bhai intervened quickly to placate him. 'Baoji, Rohan will speak to Jenny. Maybe she will agree.'

Ma suddenly said sharply. 'Remember son, once your children are older there would be no coming back. You will be forced to stay abroad and we will die without seeing your face.'

'Why are you talking of dying, Ma?' I pleaded even as she left the room, her outburst leaving a deep silence in its wake.

Baoji struggled for composure while I sat with my head bowed, looking deep into my teacup as if it would throw up an answer. After a few minutes I stood up to leave the room and said to nobody in particular. 'I will speak to Jenny.'

I felt disturbed and decided to settle the matter with Jenny during our forthcoming trip to Agra. I did not know then that this visit would be unforgettable for all the wrong reasons.

We boarded an early morning train to Agra and during the long journey Sanjay captivated other passengers with his antics while Riya spent the entire time looking in bewilderment at passing villages. Jenny snuggled up to me and, imagining her agreeing to a new life here, I visualized how happy this would make Baoji, Ma and Bhai.

We took a rickshaw from the station, soon catching our first glimpse of the Taj, our excitement growing manifold as we reached closer. The Taj Mahal, a testimony to Emperor Shahjahan's undying love for his beautiful queen Mumtaz, lay before us in a majestic glory that took our breath away.

Enchanted by the mausoleum's ethereal beauty, we sat in its garden while Riya and Sanjay played in the shallow water fountains nearby. Watching Jenny silently imbibe the pristine exquisiteness of the Taj Mahal, I felt this to be the opportune moment.

'Dear, I am so glad you are enjoying it here. Even Riya and Sanjay are so happy. Don't you agree it is time we took a decision?'

'A decision? What do you mean?'

'We are having a wonderful time here, but our holidays are getting over. We have to decide whether to move here or not.'

She hesitated before replying. 'Rohan, I really love your family, I do, but I cannot live here permanently.'

Stunned by her bluntness I struggled to respond. 'How can you say that? See how well the children have adjusted. Here they will grow up in a big, extended family while they have no one in Glendale.'

Jenny replied carefully. 'You are right about that, but don't you see what I can see clearly in everybody's eyes when they look at us?'

'What do you mean?'

'Rohan, our children and I are outsiders here. You love

us so you don't see that, but others do. Sure we will learn the language and way of life, but we will always be treated differently. Surely you will not want your wife and children to be treated as strangers in your own land.'

'But you have seen so many foreigners living happily here.'

'I certainly have, but this is my personal choice.'

'But there must be a reason! In every respect we are better off here, we will buy a bungalow and you will have servants and not have to work at all. We will live a life of luxury that we cannot even think of abroad and the kids will love being with their grandparents and cousins. So, what is the problem?'

Jenny thought long before replying. 'What you say is correct and I have no doubt you will look after us very well. I also realize how important your family is to you and how long you have waited for this to happen. But I am fearful.'

'Fearful? What is there to fear?'

'You won't understand so let's not discuss it.'

'But I insist! It can't go on like this forever. You are right I want to settle here and I must know why you don't agree.'

'OK, if you must know. But let me warn you I may not make sense for I am not too sure myself.'

Jenny took a long breath, continuing to look straight ahead at the Taj.

'You know very well I have never experienced the joy of growing up in a family, surrounded by parents, brothers and sisters. Uncle did his best that I don't miss my parents, but he traveled a lot and I lived in a hostel so it could never be the same. And then I met you. When I saw your attachment to your family it felt that through you I could fulfill my need for one. That is why I was always open to the idea of moving here and you must believe me that I came here fully prepared to commit myself, for your sake and mine. In any case, with Uncle having passed on, I cannot live in Sydney so the choice is clear to me: Glendale or here.'

Pausing to collect her thoughts Jenny continued.

'I thought I would prefer living here in a large extended family in which my children will be with grandparents, uncles, aunts, and cousins. I also have wonderful memories of our first trip here and felt I could build on them since Baoji, Ma, Bhai are so loving. Most importantly I see a contentment in you that I have never seen before and trust me that means so much to me, but...'

'Tell me dear. Why have you stopped?'

'I don't know how to say this and forgive me if I offend you. I dearly want my own home, a place my children and theirs, can call their own and this seemed perfect because it is your birthplace and your family is here. But then I realized that without you the children and I are strangers here. You are our identity and it is terrifying to imagine a single day if for some reason you are not with us. Can you visualize how we will survive if God forbid something should happen to you? Imagine our fate if we wake up one day to discover we are strangers in our own home? At that stage where will we go? On the other hand, the children are born in Glendale and belong there. Don't you agree that as parents we owe it to them to provide a home they can call their own for all time to come? This has convinced me that our future is in Glendale.'

Jenny paused and not knowing how exactly to remove her apprehension I simply held her hand and said softly. 'Let us not be hasty. With time this can be your home too.'

'Yes, anything is possible with the passage of time, but I feel it is best for us to live in Glendale and visit here regularly. I also feel you should be frank with your parents. I believe they will understand and it is far better they don't live with false hope.'

'But maybe the kids won't want to go back.'

'They are young and it's just a holiday for them.'

'Dear, please try to see it from my point of view. My parents did so much for me and now they are getting on in age it is my duty to look after them. Should a son be so selfish to desert his parents in their old age?'

I desperately reasoned with her and she listened patiently before merely pointing to where Riya and Sanjay were playing. As I turned to see, I immediately understood what she meant. They were in a sand pit surrounded by a motley group of children who were pointing at and discussing about them. Not understanding a word, they kept playing but it was clear they were being viewed with curiosity like we would an animal in a zoo.

Getting up quickly I shooed away the gaping children and brought Sanjay and Riya to where Jenny sat. At that moment Sanjay innocently asked, 'D, why were those kids pointing at us?'

I brushed aside his question and noticing this Jenny said with a laugh. 'Don't get serious and spoil this wonderful day. Look how the dark clouds are casting their shadow on the dome as if covering it with water. Oh, Rohan, this is so beautiful!'

Jenny's joy was infectious and before long I forgot the discussion that had threatened to take a serious turn. We spent the afternoon drinking in the beauty of the Taj, taking photographs to preserve our memories, and picking knick-knacks from the many souvenir shops just outside the magnificent monument.

It was evening when we boarded the Taj Mail and as the train chugged slowly out of the station, Jenny nestled her head on my shoulder, her eyes closed. I ran my fingers through her hair and said softly. 'Dear, what do you say we move here for one year and go back if you don't like it?'

As my words sank in, I felt her stiffen before she turned away without reply and in a few minutes she was fast asleep. The train sped into the enveloping darkness and in my heart I knew I had her reply.

While everybody slept, I sat awake digesting Jenny's words, desperately wanting to believe she was not correct...she just could not be. India was home to people of all countries, religions, colors and backgrounds and unlike her, most had no family here. Then remembering Sanjay's innocent question, I sadly realized this would never have arisen in Glendale. It was also true that in Canada they would never have to face the question of acceptance. At that moment I knew for sure that by marrying Jenny and living abroad so long, I had shut the door of my home upon myself.

We stayed for another fifteen days during which time the topic of relocation simmered unspoken. I somehow kept hoping Jenny would change her mind, but that did not happen. Finally on our last evening we sat down for a special meal cooked by Ma. At first everyone chatted merrily but the mood soon turned sober and a silence descended; as a family we never really knew how to say goodbye. As Ma fed us dessert, she looked ready to cry and Baoji wasn't far away. After some time Baoji asked tenderly, 'Son, this visit was too short. When will you come next?'

'Well, Baoji, Jenny and the children have really enjoyed themselves and I am sure we will be back soon, maybe in a few months.'

'That will be very good.'

Ma came and sat next to me. 'Rohan, it is so wonderful when we are all under one roof.'

'Don't worry, Ma, time will just fly and we will be back before you know it.'

'Yes, dear. As you know we are getting older and your being with us is such a comfort.'

Sensing Jenny's unease, I slowly got up. 'Ma, we will return very soon. In fact, I will send tickets so you can all visit us. You have never traveled abroad and it will be an unforgettable trip.'

'No, dear. Going abroad holds no charm for me.'

'Human life is the same everywhere,' said Baoji. 'The most important thing is for families to stay together.'

'But Baoji, to enjoy life we must have different experiences.'

'Travel does broaden the mind, but visiting a new place is not the same as permanently staying there. By leaving your home you eventually lose your culture and language and what is far worse is that the next generation will have no connection with your roots. I know these are modern times, but some truths remain unchanged and one of them is that there is no greater sin than to meet your maker in a foreign land.'

'I don't believe that,' I countered forcefully, unable to stop even though I didn't want an argument. 'If what you say is true human life would have perished long back. It is travel and migration that enriches a man's culture and helps him prosper.'

'Relax, Rohan,' Bhai stepped in. 'Baoji has his views and you have yours. No need to get so wired.'

I stood silently, feeling foolish at overreacting, as Baoji got up to lovingly embrace me. 'Son, you will remember my words when you are older. Your Ma and I will always wish you to be with us so we can die with our children and grandchildren by our side. But if you live separately, we will still be happy in your happiness.'

Ma too came forward to hold me and in their comforting embrace I felt I was a small child, warm and secure, wishing I could stop time.

'Come on,' said Bhai, patting me affectionately. 'We must sleep now since we have to leave early in the morning.'

Baoji and Ma slowly released me and as I left the room, I looked back at them one more time. Baoji had his arm around Ma, consoling her while she cried silently and my heart ached to see them so immeasurably saddened. But I was helpless.

Glendale, Ontario: **1935–1943**

Back in Glendale, time passed in a blur as Jenny and I got frightfully busy with work at home and office. Riya and Sanjay were quite a handful too. But I badly missed Baoji, Ma and Bhai and often woke up in cold sweats after a bad dream involving one of them. Some months later I would make plans to go home, saving money and accumulating leaves. It became a pattern.

Despite the troubled political landscape amidst the independence struggle, I managed to travel home once every two or three years, but for some reason always without Jenny. Each time Baoji and Ma said they understood, but Bhai confided this was when they finally gave up all hope of my return. My trips helped lessen my guilt of abandoning Baoji and Ma, yet watching the children fly kites, enjoy weddings and festivals and generally have a marvelous time often made me wonder if I had made a mistake by not putting my foot down and moving back. But it was too late now.

Children grow up fast and before I knew it their studies, summer camps, and other activities made it increasingly harder to go home. Moreover, for them, Ambala was a holiday destination albeit special and they now preferred new places. I was clearly outvoted and while my heart pined to be with Baoji and Ma, my visits became less frequent over the years.

Bhai wrote to me with unfailing regularity and I took

comfort in his letters. It surprised me greatly when he wrote about nearing retirement and fixing Maya's wedding the coming winter. It made me wonder how silently time had marched on. Had it really been that many years? It seemed like only yesterday that Bhai had got a job, got married, and Maya was born. I immediately showed his letter to Jenny, which didn't help for Bhai wrote in Urdu, and giving a quizzical look she shot back. 'What is it, Rohan? You know I can't read this.'

'I am sorry. Of course, you can't. Bhai says he is about to retire and has fixed Maya's wedding. Can you believe he is retiring?'

'Why is it so surprising?'

'Because I always think of him as a young man.'

'Do you know even you have only few years left? Also, it will soon be time for Riya too to be married.'

As Jenny's words sank in, I began thinking: indeed, I was to retire in about four years that meant Baoji was around seventy-two years old! Where had time gone? Somehow a lifetime had flown by practically unnoticed! Determining to spend more time with Baoji and Ma before God made that impossible, I wrote to Bhai that Sanjay and I would attend the wedding; Jenny and Riya were unable to fit it into their schedule.

Ambala, Punjab: 1944

My visit home was a cruel reminder that Baoji and Ma were in the sunset of their lives. They looked quite old and as they hugged me, the sharpness of their bones and frailty of their frames brought tears to my eyes. Even I was grey-haired but Ma's only comment was that I had lost weight and she immediately went into the kitchen to make my favorite sweets.

Sanjay and I spent a joyful month at home. It was bliss to wake up each morning and greet Baoji, Ma and Bhai, something I dearly missed. Sanjay thoroughly enjoyed the constant stream of people in the house and servings of hot tea and snacks. This was unimaginable in Glendale and I was happy he got a glimpse of an important part of my old life.

The wedding itself was a splendid affair attended by over 500 guests including old friends. Dressed in Indian clothes, Sanjay took part in all functions along with Saket. He was having the time of his life and I too felt good hoping that he would never forget his Indian roots. This was especially important for I had not forgotten Baoji's words that when someone married a foreigner and lived abroad that arm of the family got cut off forever. I was determined to prove him wrong.

Maya's departure seemed to empty the house of its laughter and joy, but fortunately not for long. She had not moved far and when she began coming for short visits a few days later, it felt like she had never left.

It was soon time for our return and on the last day we assembled in Baoji's room. Parting was always painful and over the years I had come to dread such moments because of a lurking fear this could be the last time I was seeing Baoji and Ma. As we chatted, Ma got up slowly with Sanjay's help and took out a small cloth bundle from her old metal trunk. With all of us looking on, she untied the bundle with shaking hands and took out a gold necklace and a pair of diamond earrings which I knew belonged to her mother. Then summoning me she said, 'Son, your Baoji and I have a family heirloom for each of our grandchildren, to be given when they marry. God willed us to bless Maya's marriage, but time is against us and we don't think we shall be fortunate to see Riya's and Sanjay's marriage.'

'No Ma, please don't say that. I will be back very soon with the entire family.'

'That will be good, but for now we want you to take this. These diamond earnings are for dear Riya and this necklace is for Sanjay's wife. Even if we are not alive our blessings will always be with you and them.'

'Ma, please give them to the children yourself when they are here next.'

Baoji stepped forward and taking the ornaments from Ma firmly pressed them into my hand while Bhai said, 'Rohan, please do as Ma and Baoji say. It will make them happy.'

Teary eyed, I hugged Baoji and Ma, promising repeatedly to be back soon. I touched their feet and Sanjay did the same. At that moment, in a small corner of my heart, I still clung to a faint hope of coming back to them for good.

Glendale, Ontario: 1945–1959

It had been a long, exhausting day at work and stepping out of the car I looked forward to a hot cup of tea, deciding to later write home for it had been a while since I had heard from Bhai. Spotting Jenny in the kitchen I asked where Sanjay and Riya were; it was getting dark earlier nowadays and I worried if they were not home on time.

'Sanjay is in his room studying for what he calls a "heavy" test tomorrow and Riya rang just now to inform she is with Janice and will be home shortly.'

'Good. And how was work?'

'Fine, but it is now strenuous for me and I may soon call it quits.'

'You wish! I can't imagine you staying home all day, you will drive the kids and me nuts!'

'Stop joking, Rohan. Look, why don't you change and I will make tea.'

I washed my face and after changing into casuals looked in on Sanjay to find him on his bed with a Math book, his favorite music playing loudly in the background. By force of habit I immediately remarked, 'Why don't you study at the table and also stop the music so you can concentrate better?'

Completely ignoring my suggestion, Sanjay merely smiled back and I left his room, remembering that in our days if Baoji caught either Bhai or me studying on the bed we would instantly get a wallop. But Sanjay refused to change; in his defense he always got top grades and I couldn't argue with that.

It was customary at our home to have tea upon return from work; I guess I had unknowingly picked this habit up from my childhood when Ma would welcome Baoji with a hot cup of tea on his return from office, something common in Indian households. Jenny was earlier not fond of tea, but in the good old days this was the time of day when Professor Hubertson and I would exchange notes. One day I made tea and a ritual was born. Now, sitting on the sofa sipping hot tea with Jenny by my side I asked again, 'So, how was your day?'

'Fine, but you are so involved in your work you are just not aware what is going on in your own house.'

'Hey! What happened? Did I miss something? You appear to be on the warpath.'

'I have been saying for so long that your daughter is no longer a child, but you still treat her like one.'

'She will always be my baby. Did anything happen? You just said she is with Janice.'

'I told you what Riya told me, but I know she is not with Janice.'

'How can that be?'

'OK I will tell you, but promise me you will not lose temper or speak to Riya about it.'

Not too sure where this was heading, I quickly promised and she continued. 'This is not the first time Riya has rung up to say she is with Janice. But today I chanced to meet Janice's mom and she said Riya has not visited them for a long time. I later spoke to Janice and gathered from her that Riya has been spending too much time with Neil, Mr Ficke's son.'

'You worry too much. Neil is a perfect gentleman and he and Riya are in the same class.'

'You always defend her, but I can see the signs. Obviously something is going on why else would she say she is with Janice when she is actually with Neil?'

Just then Riya came in along with Janice and Neil and with a carefree 'Hi Dad, Hi Mom' went to her room with her friends. I immediately whispered to Jenny, 'You were saying...'

'Maybe I do worry too much...she obviously went to Janice's house but what is Neil doing with them?'

Telling her to relax I went to my study but while I read, my thoughts went back to what she had said. Riya was a vivacious, popular girl and whether I liked it or not, boys were attracted to her. So far she was focusing on studies and her plans were laid out—she would complete post-graduation in two months and thereafter move to Ottawa to intern with a law firm. I hated to let her go, but didn't want to stand in the way of her career; the consolation was that she would not be too far and be home most weekends.

It seemed hard to believe that my baby had grown up and then a thought suddenly struck me: Jenny got married at twenty-four and even though nowadays girls married late, the time was not too far for Riya! I knew I had to do something to ensure her continued connection with her roots which meant she should not end up marrying a Canadian or American. I flung my book aside and hurried upstairs to Jenny.

Jenny laughed hysterically when I outlined my proposal. 'What age are you living in, Rohan? Riya will decide what is best for her just as we did. You better not try to match her with someone from India. On second thoughts, I would like to see you try to do that, it's going to be hilarious!'

'I am very serious. She should marry a nice Indian boy. You know marriages last a lifetime in India because the men are faithful and look after their wives very well.'

'I can vouch for that!'

'I don't plan to go to India to find her a groom but she needs a suitable boy living here in Canada or the US who has a firm grounding in Indian culture and values.'

'There is no Indian boy here except for Mr Mahajan's son and I know how much you like him!'

'Don't mention that rascal! Just think, Mahajan lived his entire life in India and moved here only a few years back and already his son introduces himself as "Sam" though his real name is Sukhvinder! And Mahajan is worse, he does not even associate with Indians! He is friends with me only because I am married to you. I am sure if given a chance he will instantly leave his village-born wife of thirty years for a white lady. Shame on such people for trying to be more Canadian than those born here!'

'Relax, dear, I only meant there are no eligible bachelors.'

'Maybe not in Glendale but there is now a sizable Indian population in Kingston, Vancouver and even Ottawa. I will immediately make inquiries.'

'But should you not first consult Riya?'

'I will, but let me first find a boy for her.'

Thus, began my quest for an Indian groom for my daughter. I had a simple yardstick: a good-looking young man with a stable job and a modern outlook, but with respect for traditional Indian values. Unfortunately, first-generation boys born in Canada scorned anything Indian and those who had recently migrated here were so anxious for acceptance they shied from anything Indian. I found this astonishing; I had lived here all my life but always took pride in my roots.

I also found it disturbing that most young men I met were keen on Riya even without meeting her. Undoubtedly she had impressive credentials, but I gathered their interest lay in her being Canadian by birth with an Indian father; the former satisfied their craze for 'foreign' while the latter took care of the sentiments of their traditional parents. Riya deserved better.

Jenny thoroughly enjoyed my endeavors, especially when I began making surreptitious visits to meet a few eligible boys. She couldn't quite understand my fixation with an Indian groom, but was too nice to protest.

I even wrote to Bhai who advised me not to impose my choice on Riya. But I had to do what I thought was best for her, though at times I would remember Baoji's words, 'settling abroad will bring a time when children marry foreigners and then that arm of the family is lost forever' and wonder if my search was indeed for her happiness or my own desperation to cling to my roots.

Time passed and Riya settled in Ottawa as planned. She was gregarious and even Sanjay, who was reserved, could not withstand her charms. Brother and sister would spend the entire day talking together, playing games, or even fighting! I often joked when I returned from work that I could instantly tell from the peaceful silence that she was out. Now, the house seemed emptied of fun and laughter and we missed her dearly, looking forward to weekends when she was back to create a happy mayhem. Having sworn Sanjay to secrecy, I could now openly discuss my efforts to find an Indian groom for Riya, which was invariably the topic at the dining table.

'Dad, I still think you should first discuss this with Riya,' suggested Sanjay, as he savored dal makhani.

'I am positive she will agree the boy I recommend is the

right choice,' I replied. I was in a particularly good mood for I had something important to share. Moreover, I was enjoying the Indian food Jenny had learned to cook from Ma.

'Sanjay is right and I have been saying the same thing for so long, but you simply won't listen,' chided Jenny.

'But just hear me out first,' I replied, taking out a photograph from my pocket and handing it to Jenny as I keenly watched her reaction. But she merely looked at it quietly and passed it to Sanjay.

'So, what do you think?' I asked, anxious for approval.

'Who is this, Dad?' asked Sanjay.

'This is Vikram. He is a doctor in Ottawa. His father is also a doctor and they belong to a respectable family of Old Delhi. Vikram came to the States some years back to study medicine and then moved here for residency. I met him the other day at Mr Mathalon's house in Kingston, and then spoke to his dad who sent this photograph. They are interested and I feel this will be a good match.'

'He is certainly good looking, but what is more important is what Riya thinks. Personally I am not sure she would like to marry a doctor,' commented Jenny.

'Dad, I don't think you should proceed without speaking to Riya.' There was an urgency in Sanjay's voice that surprised me.

'Of course, I plan to do just that when she is home this weekend. But is there something I should know?'

Sanjay didn't reply and instead concentrated on his food as if he had said nothing. Jenny finally agreed to be present when I brought up the topic of Vikram, but on the condition that she would not make a recommendation. A thought briefly crossed my mind that something was being kept from me but I tossed it aside and carefully retrieved the photo, confident that Riya would approve my choice. After all he had everything going for him: good looks, a doctor's income, and most importantly, he was Indian. I could already hear wedding bells and thankfully it would be a proper Indian wedding, which would especially please Baoji and Ma.

I wanted the day to be just perfect. I had just finished ordering few of Riya's favorite dishes from a nearby Indian restaurant when she arrived excitedly hugging all of us and cheerfully insisting Jenny get her tea. We sat together and I smiled indulgently seeing her and Sanjay joke with each other. Deciding this was the right moment, I got up to bring the photograph when Riya asked, 'Dad, where are you going?'

'I am going to my study. I have something to show you.'

I caught Jenny and Sanjay give each other a meaningful look before Riya bounced up and enthusiastically holding my arm said, 'Whatever you have can wait. First, let me show you something.'

'What is it dear?' I asked, sitting down again.

'Look here, everyone,' said Riya excitedly. Then opening her purse, she carefully took out a photograph and showing it to Jenny asked, 'What do you think, Mom?'

'Who is this?' asked Jenny, passing the photo to Sanjay who glanced at it briefly before handing it to me.

As I extended my hand wordlessly, Riya came up to me, putting her hands around my shoulders. 'Isn't he sweet, Dad?'

The photo was of a handsome youth—tall, well-built, and fair with light blue eyes and brown hair. I looked at Riya and asked, 'Who is he, is he a colleague in the firm?'

'This is Lou and I love him,' Riya said simply.

Her reply stunned me into silence; Baoji's predictions were coming true and I felt angry and helpless and struggled for control. 'But Riya you are too young for all this. Besides, how long have you known each other? Who are his parents? What do they do?'

'Relax Dad,' replied Riya, completely unruffled. 'Sanjay knows Lou. We were together in Kingston, though he was in a different major. He works for the government in Ottawa. I am positive you will like him and I want Ma and you to meet him and his family. This will make me so happy.'

Later, when we were alone, Jenny said she found it hilarious when I told Riya she was too young for marriage since I had myself been on a groom-hunt for her.

Riya and Lou got married in a beautiful Christian ceremony. Despite initial reservations and my desire for her to marry an Indian boy, I was happy to see them happy together.

Despite my best attempts, no one from home could attend the wedding; I knew I was being impractical for there were restrictions in newly independent India and Baoji and Ma were now too old to travel so far. Bhai could not leave them alone either. I felt sad they could not personally bless their granddaughter, but it comforted me to see Riya wear Ma's diamond earrings.

Riya's wedding led to few changes since she had already been staying away. However, it did make Jenny and me realize that we were not getting younger. Jenny quit her job a few months later while I began preparing for retirement; it seemed incredible that I had joined the university as a stopgap arrangement and ended up spending almost thirty years here!

Sanjay graduated and started a business consultancy firm with a friend. They rented an office in the local mall and were immediately successful. It was a relief he had no plans to leave home.

Life fell into a routine as Jenny adjusted to being at home. The monotony was broken by visits from Riya and Lou. It was wonderful to see two people so much in love and I had long back reconciled to her not marrying an Indian. For some time, I contemplated making an effort to get Sanjay an Indian bride but he flatly refused. Jenny also did not support me saying, 'I thought you would have learned when you failed with Riya.'

'What is wrong in wanting the best for your child?' I countered.

'I wonder if what you really wish is to find acceptance with Baoji and Ma. Maybe you think this will please them and they will forgive you for not living with them.'

Jenny's remarks caught me by surprise and I retorted. 'How can you say this? All I want is Sanjay's happiness. We both know that Indian girls have solid family values and make fine life partners.'

Jenny immediately softened, but her anguish lay bare when she spoke. 'Rohan, my entire life I have seen you struggle with yourself, torn between us and your family in India. Do you think it made me happy? I often thought of moving to India just to make you happy, but it would just not have worked out. You should be satisfied with the undeniable fact that through you, your family here and in India shall always be connected. All parents wish children to be near, but it is far more important to them they are happy wherever they are. Just think, are we not happy for Riya though she stays away?'

Jenny made sense, but I hurt not because Baoji, Ma and Bhai wanted me with them, but because *I* wanted to be with them. I didn't really expect her to understand.

'You are right, Jenny. We should do whatever makes Sanjay happy,' I replied, confident he would take the right decision.

A few days later Jenny told me Sanjay had confided his and Sarah's desire to get married. I knew they were good friends since college, but for some reason this surprised me. Anyway, we called Sarah's parents over for dinner and in a few days Sanjay got engaged. While everybody celebrated, I quietly slipped down to my study and wrote a long letter home. Even though Baoji and Ma had never really known their grandson and would never know his wife, it was my duty to inform them.

Sanjay and Sarah got married in the local church and we had a grand reception for them. I was relieved they had a Hindu ceremony too, much like Jenny's and mine many years ago. I knew Jenny had a hand in this, knowing how much it meant to me, and felt blessed my children would do anything to make me happy.

Jenny and I gifted Ma's gold necklace to Sarah and by this one act she was now a member of my family in India, ironically a family she would never know. If we were home Ma would have herself made Sarah wear it and blessed her, but she was thousands of miles away. Sarah could not possibly appreciate the sentiment of a stranger, but it felt good to fulfill Ma's wish.

Soon after, Sanjay moved to a nearby house and coincidently Sarah got a job in Jenny's old library. They often dropped in for evening tea or dinner and we made travel plans as I was determined to take Sarah home for a visit and she too was excited at the prospect.

Our life had come a full circle and Jenny and I were again alone in our home. I still enjoyed my job, but it was increasingly becoming an effort. Besides, it meant leaving Jenny alone so

I gave myself another year at the most. I also yearned to visit home, which was long overdue.

One day, I was in my study planning a visit home when Jenny called excitedly. 'Come quickly, look who is here!'

'Coming,' I replied and climbed up, wondering who it was since we were not expecting guests.

Entering the living room, I saw Jenny happily laughing and hugging Sarah and Sanjay. 'What is the good news? Come on, Sarah, you tell me. I can't trust either your mom or Sanjay.'

Sarah blushed. 'Dad, I'll tell you, but first eat the cake we brought.'

'Yes, Dad. First the sweets and then the news,' said Sanjay, coming towards me with a big piece of cake which he forcefully thrust in my mouth as Jenny watched indulgently.

'That's good, now please tell me the news quickly.'

'Sarah is pregnant!' replied Sanjay hugging Sarah. 'She told me just now and we rushed here to share this with Mom and you.'

'That's wonderful! Congratulations!' I shouted, happily hugging Jenny, Sarah and Sanjay. 'Why, you must tell Riya at once. She will be so thrilled.'

I immediately wrote to Bhai informing him about the good news, imagining the celebrations back home. A few days later I got a long reply wherein Bhai conveyed everybody's congratulations but also a word of caution from Ma that as per tradition the news should be kept secret. This—together with eating specific foods and offering prayers—she listed, would ensure the birth of a male child. Reading the letter transported me to the days of my youth when Jenny had been the expectant mother and Ma had given similar advice. It felt good knowing that some things never changed.

As Sanjay, Jenny, Riya and I paced the hospital hallway, Sarah delivered our grandson, a healthy nine-and-half pounds, in the early hours of a Sunday morning. Holding the tiny baby took me back many years when I held newborn Riya and felt fulfilled.

After Sarah and the baby came home from the hospital, it was clear they needed help so they moved in with us. This was supposed to be temporary, but I hoped this would continue, for both Jenny and I could just not stay away from the baby.

To hold on to my roots, I had given my children Indian names and was thankful that Jenny did not object; maybe she was compensating for not moving to India, but whatever the reason it was joyful to hear the familiar sounds all day. I hesitated to suggest the same to Sanjay and Sarah, but when they were thinking of names I could not stop myself. I was ecstatic when they picked 'Madan', dear Bhai's formal name.

Jenny, Sanjay and Riya understood a little Hindi and knowing I enjoyed hearing my mother tongue would speak few words with me. In fact, we all had a natural flair for languages and spoke or understood a dozen between us; maybe it had to do with Jenny and me living in Europe earlier where we met so many people of different nationalities. Now, holding little Madan in my arms I spoke to him in Hindi, typical affectionate words while feeding, bathing, or just enjoying his infancy.

When Madan was two months old, Sanjay and Sarah moved back to their home. Sarah rejoined work and Jenny began looking after Madan, but she found it difficult to go to their house every day. Finally, Sanjay and Sarah moved back with us, which was more practical.

Bhai and I kept up our regular correspondence and as per habit I would translate and read aloud each letter to Jenny and the children. I did this to keep them in touch with their roots, but whenever Bhai mentioned how much Baoji and Ma loved their great-grandkids, it saddened me that they had missed playing with my children and grandchildren; I felt I had robbed them of this happiness.

Saket, Bhai's son, was now a highly paid computer professional and had recently got married; I had planned to attend the wedding, but had to cancel at the last minute. Around this time Bhai wrote that Professor Hardayal was no more and Baoji had lately been keeping unwell. I immediately thought of going home, but so much was going on with little Madan's arrival that I could not firm up my travel plans.

Turning into the driveway, I slowed to let the postman exit, wondering what had brought him at this hour; he usually came in at noon and it was now around 4 p.m.

'Rohan,' Jenny called from the living room when I entered the hallway.

'Just coming,' I replied. 'Let me take off my coat.' After hanging my coat in the closet I asked, 'Yes, dear, what is it? What did the postman bring?'

Looking ashen she silently held out the paper in her hand. It was a telegram and I extended my hand, sensing its ominous nature. Its grim message registered with numbing intensity even before I read it completely for I had been dreading this news all my life, in dreams and when awake, praying it never came. At that moment, everything stood still, and in a daze I continued to look at the paper in my hand, reading and rereading the four words on it: 'Baoji is no more'. The inevitability of these words had haunted me all my life yet I could not face up to them. I felt my breath constricting, my legs become unfeeling, and then, as if from very far away, I heard Jenny cry out, 'Rohaaaan!'

I must have fainted for when I opened my eyes, I saw Jenny crying softly while fanning my face as I lay on the sofa. My fist was clenched so tight it hurt and I opened it slowly to see the fateful message crumpled. Its black words seemed to leap out at me and tears that lay bottled for a lifetime could be stopped no more.

In this faraway land I thought of Baoji, he who brought me to this world, who steadied me as I learned to walk, who laughed so loud it made everyone join in. I had prepared for this moment, but the helplessness of being thousands of miles away, unable to see Baoji, touch his feet in reverence, and seek forgiveness for forsaking him was driving me crazy with grief.

After some time, the questions came flooding in. Was it a sudden heart attack? When did it happen? Where? Who was with him at that time? Did they not rush him to hospital? But there was no one to look to for answers. Thinking of Ma and Bhai and what they must be going through I cursed myself for being so far. All this while Jenny sat beside me, joining in my grief as best as she could, but she had not really known Baoji. The pain of his death was my own to bear.

'Rohan,' consoled Jenny. 'Please have courage. What has happened has happened. We are helpless before God's will.'

Still clutching the telegram I slowly sat up with Jenny's help. In this hour of sorrow my place was at home with Ma and Bhai, but I was so far away, totally cut-off. I could not even speak to them for they had no telephone. Truly, I thought, the elders labeled a trip to a foreign land as severe punishment for most sinful of criminals, aptly named 'Black Waters' for the oceans swallowed the offender, never to return him to his mother's arms. I felt I was that offender.

Looking again, I saw the telegram bore a two-day-old date. Why, I was at a party at the time my family was facing its worst tragedy! I felt like an outsider and the permanency of death meant I could never make amends.

Jenny got up. 'Please go wash and get a grip. The children will be home soon.'

I perfunctorily washed myself and went to my study to be alone. I sat for a long time, miserable and unable to share my grief as no one here really knew Baoji and I was far from those who did. Lost in sorrowful thoughts I faintly heard the door above open and Madan run inside shouting, 'We won!' Then in the same breath, he said to Jenny, 'I'm starving! Please give me milk and cookies. Where's Granddad?'

Knowing he would rush down to tell me about his game, I immediately dried my tears. Expectedly, he came bounding down the steps and jumping right into my arms yelled excitedly, 'Grandpa, we won!' I held him tight, sad at the realization that he could never meet his wonderful great grandfather. Sensing something wrong, Madan innocently asked, 'Why are you sad?'

At that moment Jenny came down and pulling Madan away said, 'Great grandfather has passed away. Come and have cookies.'

Without saying a word Madan briefly hugged me tight before leaving. He was but a child and no one here really had a connection with Baoji or for that matter with any one in India. At that moment I realized sorrowfully that when I was no more, the tenuous bond between my families here and in India would break completely. I spent a long time trying to make sense of my life, by all accounts I was a success in every way with a loving family, but I had lost my way of life and those I loved most.

That night, as I lay in bed, Jenny asked, 'Are you going to visit home?'

'I don't know. I wish I could speak to Bhai. Everything must already be over and it will take me a week to get bookings and reach. It's so bad they don't have a telephone.'

Just then the telephone rang. 'Bhai,' I exclaimed, rushing to answer it. 'I am sure this is Bhai.'

'Hello.'

'Rohan?' a faint voice came across the oceans. It was indeed Bhai and I felt heartbroken hearing him sound so alone. My voice catching, I asked, 'Bhai, how did it happen.'

'Baoji is no more.'

'Yes, Bhai,' I replied, choked with emotion, unable to speak.

I listened with a hurting lump in my throat, struggling for control, as Bhai recounted how Baoji had suddenly collapsed while reading the newspaper and it was too late by the time the doctor reached. Knowing I could not possibly reach, they cremated him the same afternoon. As he spoke, I realized Bhai did not sound the same; he seemed to have suddenly aged.

'Bhai, I plan to come home, but it will take me at least a week.'

'Ma is still in shock and she would be happy if you come, but you will undergo so much expense. Also, there is no point in coming so far if you stay for few days only. So think carefully about it,' Bhai replied, as usual concerned about me.

'OK Bhai. I will let you know. I will send a telegram if I come or is there a telephone nearby?'

'I am calling from the post office, but Mr Sharma, our neighbour, has now got a connection. Write down his number. He is very helpful and won't mind taking a message.'

'OK, Bhai. Take good care of Ma and yourself.'

'Don't worry about us. What has happened has happened. You take care of yourself. I will soon call again.'

'Bye, Bhai,' I said and kept down the phone somewhat

consoled. We had, of course, spoken in Hindi and Jenny who understood only a little immediately asked, 'What did he say?'

'Baoji had a sudden heart attack two days back. Poor Ma and Bhai must have gone through a lot.'

'What have you decided? Are you going?'

'Let me see tomorrow. My schedule is tight right now and Bhai said there is no need if I can stay for only few days. I think he is right.'

I slept fitfully that night, dreaming of Baoji calling out to me even as he fell still holding the newspaper he was reading. I ran hard to reach him, holding my hand out to him all the time, but just falling short.

It was around 4 a.m. when I got up. Leaving Jenny sleeping soundly, I went to the basement where I sat at my desk and from its drawer took out family photos. There was one of Baoji holding me in his arms, another of him with Bhai and me, and so many more. It seemed hard to believe he was no more and in one way I was thankful I had not been a witness to his end, knowing it would have broken me to see him suffer even a little.

I took out a photograph of Baoji standing next to the guava tree in our backyard. I looked at the picture for a long time and softly caressed it. After some time, I wrote on a small slip: 'Baoji—1873 to 1956' and affixed it under the photograph. There was a poster paper just above my desk that I cleared before carefully pasting Baoji's photo in its center. Then bowing my head before it, with tears flowing, I paid my last respects. From now on this was my temple.

Dear Rohan,

It is now one month since our Baoji left us. I still cannot believe he is no more, but nobody can fight God's will and somehow we are slowly coming out of our grief. I am concerned about Ma but she is very much attached to the children and this helps distract her. Do you know that through all her pain Ma repeatedly kept asking who will look after you? Here we have each other to share our sorrow and it is sad you are so far away.

That fateful day, as I watched the cremation fires lick his pyre, I longed for you to be by my side, remembering how proudly Baoji would tell everybody that he would lead a happy retired life thanks to his two sons who would take care of him. Over the years he and Ma reconciled to you living abroad, but I wonder if parents can truly be happy when children are far away.

We are blessed to have such loving parents and I am happy I was able to serve Baoji till his last days and fortunate that Ma is still with me. But life is too short so please visit home soon for Ma's sake.

Love,
Bhai

Dear Bhai,

Baoji's demise has shaken me. I remember him day and night and at times I stretch my hand to touch him...

I wish I was home, but I am a victim of my own decisions and must suffer their consequences. Truly I gained a lot by living here with my lovely family, but have lost much more. Remember, Baoji used to say about it being a sin to live abroad? I feel I have committed the sin and am paying the price. My heart and mind are always with you and Ma, but my commitments keep me here. Maybe when I was younger and the children were small I could have moved back, but it is too late now.

Bhai, I shall come home soon and bring Ma here for some time. I am sure this will be greatly satisfying for her. I now feel I should have also brought Baoji to reassure him that his son is happy.

Please take good care of Ma and yourself.

Love,

Rohan

Baoji's passing was a defining moment, signaling the beginning of the end of the life to which I had always longed to return. I often dreamed of him calling out for me and the next moment seeing him a broken man, lamenting his son had forsaken him. I also began to feel I had betrayed Ma and Bhai by not being with them in their hour of grief.

It worried Jenny to see me lost in gloomy thoughts and she tried her best to comfort me, but it was of no use. I was the son who had deserted his parents and was responsible for breaking my family, one half of which would never know the other.

Baoji's departure naturally hit Ma the hardest and for a long time it appeared she had lost her will to live. During this time, thanks to Bhai having finally got a telephone connection, I spoke to her often, each time promising to come home at the earliest. While I tried my best, it was ultimately Bhai's love and care that helped her to cope with her loss. And then I resolved to bring Ma to Glendale.

'Jenny, I want your opinion on something important,' I said after I had just finished speaking to Ma.

'Yes, Rohan?'

'I am planning to bring Ma here. What do you think?'

Jenny quietly digested what I said before replying thoughtfully. 'I honestly don't think it is a good idea simply because it will not make Ma happy. She is quite old and has never moved out of her house before. She is too set in her ways and even this climate is harsh for her. Anyway, I don't think she will agree and Bhai too will not send her so far.'

'Can you not imagine her joy on seeing her son's world here? All her life she has satisfied herself with our photographs or from what I describe in letters or over phone, but it is not the same as actually living day to day with us. I am sure it will be very fulfilling for her.'

'But even if you convince her, what about Bhai? Will she agree if Bhai objects?'

'Bhai will surely agree. He knows how much happiness this will give me and he will never deny me.'

'Do you think it is fair to ask an old woman to leave her home for an unknown place?'

'But this is not an unknown place. It is her son's home.'

We argued at length and finally realizing my mind was made up, she left the final decision to me saying, 'Your Ma is always welcome here. I just don't think it is good for her and I am sure Bhai will convince you what I am saying is right.'

Jenny was absolutely correct. Both Ma and Bhai straightaway rejected my proposal. But I stubbornly persisted, and finally, after few months of persuasion through letters and telephone calls, Ma gave in. This upset Bhai considerably and knowing Ma would not come if he did not agree I asked her to speak to him. Poor Bhai had no chance since he had never disobeyed Ma, but he made me promise that she would not stay for more than a month and I quickly agreed. Coincidently, my neighbour Mahajan was visiting his village near Ambala and happily took the responsibility to escort her. Bhai initially objected to this arrangement but I managed to persuade him and he grudgingly agreed.

My excitement grew with each passing day as I received updates about Ma's preparations; her passport was ready and Bhai confirmed he had received the ticket I sent for her. We readied Riya's room for her and everyone prepared to welcome her. Finally, the day arrived and I spoke to Ma before her departure.

'Ma, you will have a wonderful time. Make sure you look around and enjoy each minute of your flight. Mahajan will look after you well and there is nothing to worry.'

'Yes, son. But I am scared of flying.'

'Don't worry Ma. You will enjoy it a lot.'

'Wait a minute, Bhai wants to say something.'

'Yes, Bhai?'

'Rohan, Ma is going out for the first time and you have to take good care of her. See she gets her own food and keep her protected from cold. Also, ring me immediately when she reaches.'

'Yes, Bhai. Don't worry at all.'

Thus, almost fifty years after I had journeyed abroad, Ma became the second member of my family to travel abroad.

Jenny, Riya and I were at the airport to receive Ma. I was nervously pacing the arrival hall long before the flight landed and ran to hug her the moment I saw her coming out with Mahajan, unable to stop crying upon remembering Baoji. Then Jenny touched her feet in the traditional Indian greeting, bringing a smile to Riya, and Ma embraced them both.

Ma had last seen Jenny as a young woman and Riya as a child yet they were immediately comfortable. It was especially beautiful to see Ma with Riya, two very different persons yet bound by undeniable ties of blood and love. I couldn't help but think that even though they were a generation apart and lived different lives anyone could easily tell they were family. And then turning to me, Ma said, 'I am so glad I came. This is what being a family is about. When Riya speaks to me her words sound strange, but I feel the love in them.'

On the journey back Jenny drove while I showed Ma the sights and she whispered. 'This is a journey of wonderment to a fairy land, one I could never have imagined in my wildest dream.'

At home, Sanjay, Sarah and Madan were waiting in the driveway, and they greeted Ma joyously. As she lovingly held little Madan, I said, 'Is he not Sanjay's duplicate?'

Ma turned to me and replied, 'He is your carbon copy.'

Over the next few days I took Ma all over Glendale, feeling wonderful to familiarize her with what was an intimate part of my life; happy to see me so relaxed Jenny was content to let me monopolize her. Indeed, I was having the best time of my life, feeling fulfilled to see and talk to Ma all day or to simply know she was in the next room just a few feet away.

I was apprehensive how things would be managed when I was away to office since Jenny and the kids knew only few words of Hindi. So, on my first day at work I rang up a dozen times to check, but I need not have bothered and on return I found everybody enjoying the delicious Indian food Ma had cooked. It was clear that Ma and Madan were now the two most favorite persons at home.

Ma had been with me for a month now and despite her age coped well with the change. But winter was approaching earlier than usual and I worried. Bhai too faithfully rang up every day to insist she be brought back. Moreover, as the days got shorter and temperatures began dropping sharply, it appeared Ma was becoming withdrawn. Then one day at work I got a call from Jenny that shook me.

'Rohan, I think you should come home.'

'Why, what happened. Is Ma fine?'

'She is fine, but it is better you come now.'

Not understanding, I rushed home to find Jenny in the living room. 'Why did you call me? Where is Ma? Is she fine?'

'Relax, I said she is OK. But in the afternoon I took her to your study where she spent considerable time seeing Baoji's photograph. Then she straightaway went to her room and when I looked in on her later, she had packed her bag. Upon my asking she began insisting on going home immediately, so I called you.'

'Why did you take her to my study? So far I avoided doing that for she could slip on the steps and hurt herself.'

'But she didn't, did she? Forget what happened, it is more important to find out what she wants.'

I went to Ma's room to find her sitting on the bed simply gazing without focus, her suitcase neatly packed. Noticing me enter she looked at me and I asked her softly. 'Ma, are you OK?'

'Rohan, I want to go home.'

'Why so soon, Ma?'

'I have had a wonderful time, but it is time to return.'

'Stay for another month. I will take you back before winter sets in.'

'No, son. I must go now.'

'Why all of a sudden, Ma?'

'If you must know, I don't want to die here in a foreign land away from your Baoji.'

Her answer stunned me into silence; I knew this was the effect of her having seen Baoji's photo. We spoke at length, but her mind was set and finally when she began to get agitated, I promised to take her back without delay.

Leaving Ma, I immediately rang up Bhai hoping he could convince her to stay a bit longer but he too was adamant that she be brought home immediately. 'Rohan, please understand Ma can never be truly happy outside her home. You will never be able to forgive yourself should anything happen to her there, so bring her home where she belongs.'

The mere thought of Ma leaving made me dread I would never see her again. But I had no option.

On the day of her departure everyone gathered to say farewell, giving Ma small gifts as she blessed them. Madan, who had become extremely attached, was distraught and Ma too was unhappy but then she was returning home. Finally, I escorted her out and after Sanjay placed her small suitcase and mine in the car we left for the airport.

It was a long flight, taxing for Ma at this age, but she made no fuss. Having overcome my unhappiness about her leaving, I excitedly looked forward to being home after many years. Bhai received us at the airport and the moment we entered home I thought of Baoji. This was the first time he was not there to receive me; the old life had changed forever.

I stayed for ten days, feeling good to see Ma settle in her familiar surroundings. On the day I was leaving Ma called me aside. 'Rohan, I see you carrying a lot of pain. I know you tried to live your life first for Baoji and me and then for Jenny and your children, but never for yourself. Now I want you to go back contended. You have done your duty as a son. If you want me to be happy you must promise to stop living in the past.'

I flew back in a contemplative mood. Ma's words had made me realize it was time to appreciate the present.

I do not honestly remember any other time I was so relaxed; even Jenny and the kids commented on this. Ma's visit had endorsed my life choices and I felt an inexplicable comfort sensing her presence in every room. Jenny and I began enjoying life as we did in our twenties—dining out and visiting new places. Ma's counsel had resolved my lifelong dilemma and I was at peace, thanking God for my wonderful family that always stood by me despite my obvious preoccupation with those in another land. But it was too good to last. Bhai informed that Ma was now frequently unwell and my focus shifted again.

While I had last spoken to Ma assuring her she would get better, I knew she was giving up when she replied with difficulty. 'Why should I live? I have seen my children and grandchildren. I first lived for my parents, then my husband, then my sons, but now I wish to die for myself.' And then she added, almost in a whisper. 'I am only waiting for you, son. I will die happy once I see you one last time.'

When Bhai informed me that the writing was on the wall, I held back from rushing to her, believing that once we met, Ma would give up her tenuous hold on life.

Ma's words haunted me day and night and even as Bhai's

messages became more urgent I hesitated; how could a son ever say goodbye to his mother? But when one day Bhai said she was slipping away, I booked my ticket with a sinking heart. I had to see her one last time, for her sake, and mine.

Ambala, Haryana: 1960

Bhai tried to prepare me during the drive home. 'Rohan, Ma is bedridden and floats in and out of consciousness; at times she does not even recognize me. All we can do is to pray for her.'

My eyes welled up and I looked out of the window to hide them. Bhai was grief-stricken, but he appeared reconciled; maybe it was because I lived away that I struggled to accept the situation.

Despite attempts to prepare myself, I was shocked to see Ma semi-comatose and so frail that she didn't look like herself, but then she briefly opened her eyes and in that instant I saw all her love for me. My presence did not register long and she shut her eyes again even as I softly caressed her face, repeatedly pleading, 'Ma, open your eyes. I am back, your Rohan is back.' But there was no reaction and helplessly I turned to Bhai who consoled me. 'You must be strong. At times, she even speaks a few words.'

Over the next few days Ma barely opened her eyes, but I felt she knew I was with her. Despite all possible care and precautions her restricted movements caused painful bedsores that had to be washed, cleaned and disinfected regularly. Her body was wasting with each laboured breath yet she did not complain and instead shielded her children from pain.

It was clear Ma's condition was rapidly deteriorating and I

wanted to immediately move her to a hospital, but Dr Sharma vetoed the idea. He felt, and Bhai concurred, that in her last days Ma needed only the comforting love of her family.

I was at Ma's side throughout, intermittently feeding her insipid liquids or soup, but the doctor advised anything else would cause more harm than good. So, as she lay on her propped up pillow, I spoon fed her thinking how life had come a full circle. Once a child, spoon-fed by her mother, she had grown, married, spoon-fed her children, and now in her old age she was again being spoon-fed, albeit by her children. It saddened me yet I felt blessed to be by her side, something God had denied me in case of Baoji.

Sometimes, Ma would suddenly open her eyes to say a few garbled words before falling back into a stupor. At other times, she spoke softly but coherently, something about her childhood, Baoji, Bhai and me. She appeared to be reminiscing about a time when Bhai and I were children and it was particularly sad to hear her speak of Baoji in the present tense. When this happened, Bhai and I would look at each other and then away, helpless in the face of old age and painfully aware of its end result.

A month had passed and I rang Jenny daily to check how she and the kids were doing and update her on Ma's condition. Then, one day after I had just finished talking to her, Bhai called me to his room.

'Rohan, what have you decided about going back? Jenny must be finding it difficult.'

'I can't leave Ma, my place is here with her.'

'I understand, but how long can you stay? Your family needs you too.'

'I can stay some more, Jenny is fine.'

'You heard Dr Sharma. Ma can be like this for months. Can you stay that long?'

'I'll go back when Ma is better.'

'You know in your heart that will not happen. How long must she suffer? I pray God takes her away early.' Bhai suddenly got up and left the room, his emotions tearing him apart; Ma's condition had conspired to make him helpless.

That evening, while I watched over Ma I found it ironic and sad that I had stayed away most of her life when she needed me, and come back to tend to her when she did not even know I was by her side. I felt helpless watching Ma slip away from me. My efforts at redemption were ill-timed. My love had become redundant.

Over the next few days Ma's condition remained especially worrisome. I developed a macabre fascination of watching her breathe, a shallow rasping intake, followed by a perceptible stillness and soft whispered exhalation, so quiet at times I missed it completely till in rising panic I heard her breath again.

That night, Bhai spoke to me again. 'Your presence is a comfort, but I can see its toll on you.'

'I don't know if Ma even knows I am here.'

'I am sure deep in her heart she knows her favorite child is with her and she is happy.'

'You really believe that?'

'Yes, I do. When she was better scarcely a day passed when she did not mention you.'

'She must have really missed me.'

'Yes, no mother can forget her children.'

'Bhai, I always thought I would return, but kept postponing it until one day I simply could not. Anyway, I honestly believe I made the right decision for Jenny and the children, but sadly it meant I could not be with you, Baoji and Ma. All my life I have felt torn between my two families.'

Bhai replied thoughtfully. 'When you first went abroad, dawn was breaking when we came back home after leaving you. I was in our room and heard Baoji consoling Ma who was crying uncontrollably. After some time, I heard a strange sound and realized with a start Baoji was crying and asking Ma to assure him you would indeed return. That was the only time I have heard him cry. I understood then that by letting you go they had robbed themselves of their own happiness in exchange for your bright future.'

'But I really didn't plan to stay abroad, it just happened.'

'Baoji and Ma always hoped for both their sons to be with them in their old age. Later, they wanted you here not for themselves but because they genuinely believed your happiness lay here, in your land. They reconciled when they saw you happy with Jenny.'

'But then why do I always feel I let them down?'

'You should know a parent's love is the most unselfish of all. Their child's happiness overrides every other wish including that they stay with them. This is how it has always been and how it will be. So don't feel you let them down.'

I was not entirely convinced, but somehow felt better. Then realizing it was time for Ma's food we both went to her room. As I took a spoon of dalia, Bhai supported her. 'Ma, open your mouth and eat something, then you can sleep again.'

As I brought the spoon closer to her mouth, Ma suddenly opened her eyes to look at me with an amazing clarity that shocked me even as I desperately said, 'Ma, it's me, your Rohan.'

And then, Ma whispered weakly. 'Rohan, I am glad you're here. Your Baoji will be so happy.'

Equally amazed, Bhai cupped Ma's face in his hands and said, 'Ma, both your sons are here to take care of you.'

We moved closer as she weakly whispered, 'Madan, I am blessed.'

Seeing her slip away again I shook her gently and spoke urgently, 'Ma, open your eyes.'

'It's no use, Rohan,' consoled Bhai, placing his hand on my shoulder as Ma shut her eyes. 'Let her rest.'

That night, I had a restful sleep for the first time since coming home. Knowing Ma knew I was with her made all the difference.

Ma's present comatose state made me wonder if I had imagined her speaking to me. Sitting by her side I began to play a game, counting numbers and placing a wager with myself on which count she would open her eyes and speak. I lost all bets.

Jenny was now feeling the strain of my absence and my work was suffering too. The situation was at a breaking point, but I could not bring myself to leave Ma. Aware the vigil was taking its toll, one evening Bhai asked, 'Rohan, do you think Ma is improving?'

'No, Bhai. But if she suddenly wakes up like the last time, she will look for me.'

'We are in a losing battle. You cannot be here indefinitely. You have a responsibility towards Jenny and your family.'

'I know,' I replied in anguish. 'But how can I leave Ma?'

'You have done your best. I am here to look after her now. Please go to Jenny and your children. That is what Ma would have wished.'

The very next day Jenny informed me that the university would serve me with a notice of termination unless I joined within a week. I was, of course, retiring shortly but after a lifetime of service, this meant loss of face and a huge financial blow. It was a heart-wrenching decision but I had no choice.

On the day I was leaving, I entered Ma's room to find her sleeping peacefully like a child and sat silently beside her. Caressing her soft, wrinkled face, I prayed long and hard for her, my eyes welling up with memories of the times Baoji, Ma, Bhai and I had enjoyed as a family. Knowing she lay dying, it appeared human life was meaningless, but I also knew what sustains us was knowing that our children and theirs lived on after us, and in their likeness we continued to walk the Earth long after passing on. I sat by her side for a long time knowing that once I left, I would never see her again.

'Rohan,' Bhai called softly. 'We must leave now.'

'Yes, Bhai,' I replied and then once more tenderly touched Ma's face as she slept, unaware that her son was leaving her to face her maker.

I bent down with folded hands, touched her feet and suddenly could no longer control myself. My body shook as my heart wrenched with sorrow. As Bhai rushed to hold me in his arms, I cried aloud, unwilling and unable to let go. 'Don't, Rohan. Don't hurt yourself. We are helpless before the Almighty. Just pray for Ma's suffering to end.'

Bhai guided me out of Ma's room and my last sight was of her asleep, an angelic expression on her face. I paused, for it appeared she would get up that instant, rested and refreshed.

Glendale, Ontario: 1960–1991

My thoughts were with Ma throughout the long journey home. I was sad but somewhat satisfied having been able to tend to her.

I reached exhausted but was comforted to see Jenny and Madan at the airport. Her welcoming smile instantly made me forget my tribulations and when Madan jumped, gleefully shouting, 'Granddad, Granddad,' I felt invigorated in a flash. In Ambala I had often mulled whether I had made the correct choice by settling in Canada but now, looking at Jenny and holding my grandson in my arms, my doubts were gone. This was home.

During the drive back Madan entertained me with his sweet talk as Jenny drove. After some time I noticed she was rather quiet. Suddenly something struck me as a little odd. 'You haven't once asked about Ma?'

'I am just happy to have you back. We'll talk at home.'

We turned into the driveway and I saw Sanjay's car; Jenny had told me he was busy at work, but I guessed he couldn't wait to meet me. As I got out, Sanjay came and hugged me tight. 'Hi Dad, good to have you back. How are you doing?'

'Fine, son,' I replied while Madan jumped out of the car and rushed to Sanjay; I always found it fascinating to watch them together, they were so much alike and strangers often remarked that both took after me! As Sanjay took out my suitcase from the boot, Sarah came into the driveway. 'Hi, Dad, welcome back.'

'Thanks, dear. It's good to be back and it was so nice to hear Madan speak Hindi. I thought he would have forgotten all I taught him instead he has learned new words!'

'I taught him, Dad,' replied Sanjay. 'He loves it.'

After I freshened up, we sat for a meal Jenny had especially prepared to welcome me back. Everyone knew Ma was in a bad shape and I noticed they delicately avoided her topic. All this while my thoughts were with her and I was waiting for it to be morning in India so I could speak to Bhai. Feeling tired I retired early and Jenny came up to me and said, 'I think you should call Bhai now.'

'Yes, dear. I was just wondering about the time in India right now, it should be early morning and Bhai would have woken up to look in on Ma.'

'Before you do that I want to tell you something.'

'What is it?' I suddenly felt panic surface.

'Rohan, Bhai rang just before I left for the airport to pick you. Ma is no more. I thought it better not to break the news till you rested and felt stronger.'

I had anticipated this tragedy, but Jenny's words hit me like a tidal wave. I started weeping uncontrollably as Jenny held me tight. Just then the phone rang and I intuitively knew it was Bhai. Jenny silently handed it to me and I heard Bhai's sad voice on the other end, 'Rohan, be brave. Ma went in her sleep.'

Bhai and I spoke and cried together for a long time. After seeing me off he had gone to Ma's room to find her no more. Since there was no way to tell me, he had completed the formalities and all that was now left was to visit Haridwar to immerse her ashes in the holy Ganges. Consoling me as a father would a child, he repeatedly assured me, 'Everyone must go one day and I believe Ma went peacefully.'

'Yes, Bhai. I only wish I had stayed home to look after Baoji and Ma.'

'Don't torture yourself. They were happy for you and it didn't matter where you stayed.'

'Are you alright? What did Bhai say?' Jenny asked after I kept down the phone.

'He said Ma passed away peacefully.' Just saying these words brought to mind my frail mother who had spent her entire life waiting for me and tears began to flow again till completely exhausted I slept in Jenny's arms.

Next morning as soon as I opened my eyes the sadness came flooding back. It seemed unreal; I now had no father and mother. They were gone, leaving behind only memories, and unfortunately I had only very few because I had stayed away. Bhai's remark that he felt satisfied having looked after Baoji and Ma made me dearly wish I could feel the same.

I wound my way to my study and looked at Baoji's fading photograph on my wall of remembrance before taking out Ma's photograph from an album. It was taken just a few months back when she had visited us here. Looking at her smiling face in the picture, it was hard to imagine she was no more. I was glad she had seen my world, but the wound of her departure was fresh and it hurt when I affixed her photo next to Baoji's and wrote 'Ma—1875 to 1960' underneath it. My eyes dried after some time, but the pain in my heart would remain forever.

I slowly picked up the threads of my life again. Bhai and I kept up our correspondence, sharing our joys and sorrows. A few months later Bhai wrote to me regarding the legalities of our home in Ambala. After Baoji, the house had belonged to Ma, Bhai and me and now, after Ma, it was Bhai's and mine and he outlined the options: sell our home and share the money equally, which would force Bhai to live in a smaller house or he could pay me my share and continue to live in it. I knew Bhai had modest means and could hardly afford my share and the alternative would deprive him of his home.

I pondered long, but confident that I was making a morally correct decision, one that would please Baoji and Ma, I wrote to Bhai gifting him my share, secure I would still have a home to return to.

Post retirement, Jenny and I settled into a slow-paced routine. My thoughts were often with Bhai, but it was now difficult to travel. Moreover, he had begun keeping unwell and I shied from seeing him in this condition, preferring instead the warmth of his voice over the phone for then it appeared he was the same strong big brother who had sheltered me all my life.

'Bhai, you say you are not well but you sound wonderful, as if you are still in your twenties.'

Bhai gave a hearty laugh. 'Do you know while we age, the voice does not change at all?'

'Yes, and I am happy for it helps me remember you as I saw you last—strong and healthy. Remember the corner shop? The halwai at Agrawal Sweets saying you can outeat anyone in town? Just thinking of his sweets makes my mouth water!'

'I still love sweets but do you know the doctor has advised

me to cut down on them? Can you imagine he really thinks I will! These doctors know nothing. I cannot digest my food unless I have my daily sweet!'

'We both have a sweet tooth like Baoji. Remember when there was no dessert, Ma would mix some sugar in yogurt for him? Since we don't get Indian sweets here, I do the same. Even though I have been away so long I still miss life back home, especially the foods and the language. The children speak a bit of Hindi, but it's not the same in their accent, though I feel good when they try. I really look forward to our conversations in our own language, the sweetest language on Earth.'

'Food and language are important, but not as important as one's family. You are lucky to have a loving family.'

'You are right. I am blessed and wouldn't wish to change anything if we are born again except to be together more.'

'Don't start again! There are some things on which we have no control.'

'You are right, Bhai, but I do wish I had stayed in my own land with my family.'

'Even now you are with your loving family. And we may be far but you are always in our hearts and thoughts. You owe it to yourself and your family to enjoy life where you are.'

Bhai was correct as usual and while I remained nostalgic about Ambala, I no longer despaired like earlier. Jenny and I were enjoying newfound companionship in our advancing age and I was content with my life revolving around family and Bhai's letters and phone calls.

Dear Bhai,

I have not received your letter for some time. I do hope all is well.

For quite some time I am planning to institute a scholarship in Baoji and Ma's names for poor children at our old school—B.D. High School. It was thanks to our school that we achieved success. Deserving children will get essential help and the memory of Baoji and Ma will also be kept alive. What do you think?

One more thing: last time we spoke you sounded weak. I hope you are taking your medicines regularly and maintaining a good diet. Please don't neglect your health.

I am planning to visit home with the entire family this Diwali for it is important for my children to keep in touch with their roots. I will let you know my final programme soon.

Take care,

Rohan

PS: Jenny always asks why we write letters when it is far easier to talk on phone. I tell her of the joy of touching a letter that has been in your hands, the thrill of slowly running my fingers on each word you write, and seeing and reading my own language. I also tell her that despite a lifetime abroad, speaking and hearing a different language I still 'hear' my thoughts in our native language. Somehow, holding your letter I feel I am still with you and never left home. But I don't think she quite understands.

I never got a reply from Bhai. A few days later, just when I was about to call him, the ringing telephone shattered my peace. It was Saket and the moment I said 'Hello' he began crying and I knew my worst fear had come true: dear Bhai was no more. He passed away from a silent heart attack, closing his eyes as if he was going to sleep. Saket asked if I would attend the funeral, but I did not have courage to face this cruel reality.

Fate and time had conspired to rob me of my home and family. Heartbroken, I found refuge in my makeshift temple to which I now added Bhai's photograph. I spent long hours looking at Baoji, Ma and Bhai's pictures, reliving memories of a life that was once mine.

Bhai's departure permanently closed the door on my return home because I preferred the memories of the past to the emptiness of the present. Everything was different and though there were nephews, nieces and others in Ambala, Baoji, Ma and Bhai would never welcome me. My home was lost forever to me.

The abrupt stoppage of my lifelong correspondence with Bhai served to accentuate my loss. I did ring home a few times, but I had been away so long and it hurt when a grandchild would answer and ask who I was. By and by I stopped calling, though it gave me great pleasure to receive random calls from Saket, who would respectfully invite me home.

Once I overcame Bhai's tragedy, I no longer woke up in a cold sweat in the middle of the night after a bad dream involving Baoji, Ma or Bhai. And when the phone rang, I picked it normally instead of either rushing towards it or shying away in fear it was the harbinger of ill news. But I missed them dearly.

Barely noticeable things such as feeling cold while everyone else complained of warmth were gentle reminders that old age was upon us. Jenny and I now restricted our visits to local friends or the library. Sanjay sometimes took us to Riya in Ottawa, but that too now seemed very far. Moreover, the once familiar city was now overpowering and it felt good to be in Glendale where everything was familiar and comforting.

The ardour of youth transformed into a comfortable companionship and I would often look at Jenny as she slept by my side and thank God for her. I could not contemplate life without her and, though I knew it was cowardly, prayed death claimed me first. She could always read my deepest thoughts and at such moments would comfort me, promising never to leave me alone. But she broke her pledge.

The particular day was frigid with temperatures around −30°

and the storm showed no sign of abating. Heavy snow had shut down the entire city and the television incessantly warned everyone to stay indoors. But ignoring everything Sarah left to pick up important papers from her office saying she would be back soon and the next thing we knew, the storm worsened.

I sat with Jenny, who had been running fever for the last few days, when Sanjay looked in. 'Dad, I have to go pick Sarah, she just called that her car has stalled.'

'Don't be silly. Just look outside, nobody can go out in this storm. Let it subside first.'

Peering outside Sanjay replied, 'It's not that bad. I'll be back in no time.'

'No Sanjay,' I said firmly. 'It is dangerous to drive at this time. Wait some more.'

'But Dad,' he protested. 'She says there is no heating and she is alone. You know I am a safe driver.'

As we argued, Jenny's condition worsened. She was burning with fever and when I looked closely, her face seemed bloodless. Immediately asking Sanjay to call the doctor, I held her hand.

Sanjay came back in a few minutes. 'I am afraid I can't get through to Dr Paul, I think his phone is down and he doesn't carry a mobile. It was on the news that power too is disrupted in many places.'

'Son, I have never seen your mom in such a bad state. Keep trying Dr Paul.' Then turning to Jenny I tried to make her open her eyes, but she seemed in a stupor and did not respond.

Just then the phone rang and Sanjay ran to pick it. It was Sarah. After speaking to her he came up to me. 'Dad, I am going to bring Sarah.'

'But how can you leave your mom in this condition!'

'Dad, please calm down. Dr Paul lives right next to the library and after picking Sarah I will bring him here to see Mom. Don't worry, I will be back in no time.'

Just then Jenny groaned, clearly taking a turn for the worse and I frantically gestured to Sanjay to leave, watching him step out into the blustering storm and disappear into the thick, white blanket.

The clock ticked on and I quietly got up to first try Sanjay's phone and then Sarah's, receiving no reply from both. I peered out of the window, but visibility was almost zero. Just then the phone rang and I rushed to it, anxiously asking, 'Sanjay?'

It was a relief to hear his voice. 'Yes, Dad. I have picked Sarah and I am right now with Dr Paul. His phone line is indeed down. We are starting shortly, but it may take us some time, as I will have to drive very slowly. I hope Mom is better.'

'I am really worried, she appears to be in deep sleep and her breathing is shallow. Please come as soon as possible.'

'OK Dad, you be with Mom. See you soon.'

Returning to Jenny I softly caressed her face. Holding her frail hand in mine I desperately prayed my love became well again, knowing my life was meaningless without her.

Time passed slowly. Jenny thankfully continued to sleep, though still burning with fever. Thinking of looking in on Madan who was asleep in his room, I slowly began taking my hand out of hers when she opened her eyes and said faintly, 'Promise you will be strong.'

'Hush, please rest.'

'I love you.'

'I love you too. Dr Paul will be here soon and you will be fine.'

'Please hold me, dear.'

Holding Jenny, it struck me how weak my beautiful girl had become. I kissed her softly on her forehead and looking at me intently she slowly closed her eyes.

It was a tense twenty minutes before Sanjay reached. I quickly opened the door and while Sarah went to look in on Madan, Dr Paul, Sanjay and I rushed to Jenny. Before entering her bedroom, I cautioned Dr Paul. 'She is very weak so it may be better to not wake her.'

Jenny was sleeping exactly as I had left her. Dr Paul took out his stethoscope and approached her and Sanjay too went to her while I stood back. I saw Dr Paul place his instrument on Jenny and a puzzled look came over his face. He then immediately placed his fingers on the vein in her neck and after that checked her eyes. At that moment Sanjay exclaimed loudly, 'Mom, wake up!'

It failed to register that Dr Paul had stood up wordlessly and I anxiously whispered to Sanjay, who was now holding Jenny, 'What are you doing? I asked you to not wake her.'

'Dr Paul, what is wrong with Mom,' Sanjay cried in panic. 'She is not opening her eyes.'

'Leave her, I told you she is sleeping.' I almost shouted, alarmed at Sanjay's reaction. Dr Paul came up to me, placed his hand on my shoulder said sympathetically. 'I am sorry. We are too late.'

Dr Paul's words resounded in my ears with numbing cruelty even as Sanjay continued to desperately shake Jenny, crying for his mother. But Jenny did not open her eyes.

Cold panic gripped me deadening my senses. I slowly walked over to Jenny and softly caressed her face, ignoring Sanjay who was wailing loudly. She was ice cold and for some reason I whispered, 'Her fever has broken, she is fine now.'

⸙

The storm raged all night and winds howled outside while Sanjay, Sarah, Madan and I struggled in our own ways to cope with our loss. Sanjay and Sarah slowly took charge and good neighbours came in to help. I stayed all night with Jenny, crying to God to take me too, but He willed otherwise.

By early morning the storm abated and our house filled with sympathizers as word of the tragedy spread. Someone called a priest and when he came into the bedroom Sanjay took him aside before gently guiding me to his room despite my protests.

⸙

Religion disinterested me ever since I was a child, despite Ma being a stickler for daily prayers. Baoji too displayed marked detachment, limiting his interest to the tasty prasad. Whenever Ma failed to cajole me to join in prayer she would blame him for setting a bad example. Considering that Baoji ran the house with an iron hand, it surprised me to see that he received her criticism silently. It was evident Ma held the upper hand in religious matters. Luckily, she could count upon Bhai to assist her, which gave me some respite.

When Jenny and I fell in love, our different religions were the last thing on my mind as she too was not a serious practitioner. Love ruled our hearts and our urgent marriage ensured religion remained a non-issue. Glendale had no temple and whenever we went to one in Ottawa, I would rush to get the tasty prasad while Jenny admired the architectural beauty. Likewise, visits to churches were for social events like marriages and baptisms; Riya and Sanjay were equally comfortable in a temple or church.

One Sunday, after Mrs Brown stepped in briefly to tell Jenny about the church service, I found her in a contemplative mood and nudged her softly. 'Hey, where are you lost?'

She looked thoughtful when she asked, 'Would it be fine to attend service?'

'I didn't know you wished to. Do you want to?'

'I have lately been thinking what will happen when I meet my maker.'

'Don't say that, dear. We are going to be together a long time and I will be by your side when we meet our maker. Just let me do the talking!'

Jenny ruffled my hair playfully. 'But our Gods are different, no?'

'What do you mean?'

'Well, as a Hindu you believe in life after death so I don't think we will end up together.'

'Well, Hindus believe two people in love will be together for at least seven lifetimes. So beware, you won't be rid of me in a hurry!'

Then holding her hand, I said seriously. 'We are together in this life and beyond. Anyway, I believe religion is man-made and everyone's heaven and hell are here on Earth. But if there is indeed a God, there can only be one so there can only be one heaven also.'

'But what if there is one for Christians and another for Hindus? I don't want us separated.'

'Then I will immediately apply for relocation to your heaven!'

My attempt at alleviating her mood fell flat and Jenny replied sharply. 'I can never expect a serious discussion with you!'

After a moment she added, 'But if there is a heaven surely I must be a good Christian to enter it for I know no other way.'

'So that is why you wish to attend service! You know I will not join you because I believe that neither church or temple is necessary to contemplate God.'

Jenny looked at me deeply. 'I agree and I would rather be with you than in church by myself.'

'By the way, if you really want us to be together then why take a chance? Become a Hindu!' I teased.

Jenny smiled. 'Believe me I considered that too, but your God may not accept me for He will know my reason is selfish. I will take my chances with my God and pray there is one heaven in which we are forever together.'

The conversation was getting morbid and I stood up. 'Come, let us go for a walk.'

Jenny put her hand in mine. 'Promise me one thing, dear.'

'Yes?'

'Promise you will always be with me.'

Looking deep into her eyes I gave my solemn word: 'I will always be with you, in this life and beyond.'

Jenny did not mention going to church again, but after a few days I insisted and she agreed. Not that I was changing my views but I wanted to make her feel good and if this helped, I was all for it.

We began visiting our neighbourhood church every Sunday, and it was a joy to see Jenny visibly more relaxed. But the novelty soon wore off and I began to plot ways to stop without hurting her feelings. I need not have bothered for one day she suddenly announced she would no longer attend service.

'Why, dear, it made you so happy.'

'My not going to church does not mean I will stop praying that God keeps us together in life and in heaven.'

'There you go again! Why do you talk of death so often? We are in good health and have many more years together.'

Jenny never returned to church, but on each marriage anniversary she made me renew my promise to never leave her, in life and in death.

'Dad, are you alright?'

Sanjay's words jolted me back to reality and seeing Jenny lying lifeless in front of me seared my heart. My love was no more, but then, between tears and pain, I realized that I was alive; it seemed impossible but I was breathing, my heart was beating, and being in the same position for so long was cramping my muscles. Through teary eyes I told Sanjay of my decision.

Jenny was buried in the local cemetery under the shade

of the white star magnolias. A Christian farewell was my way of saying 'thank you' to her for choosing to live her life with me.

With Jenny's departure life seemed to stand still. I never quite got used to not finding her by my side on waking up or hearing her speak or touching her. Things that went unnoticed earlier, like her doodling or her earrings or just about anything connected with her, now brought me to a standstill. I would often feel her presence so strongly that I reached out to hold her but there was a nothingness that broke my heart. I felt her in everything and would bury my nose in her clothes and take a deep breath so she could forever rest deep inside me. What hurt most was to see her smiling photo, now placed next to those of Baoji, Ma and Bhai, that took me back to our joyous times together and accentuated my wound. My entire life, I had lived with an almost morbid fear of losing Baoji, Ma and Bhai but never imagined life without Jenny. Now, alone and surrounded by photographs of loved ones on my wall of remembrance, I fervently prayed death claim me.

The harsh winter had exacted its toll and now gave way to spring, so full of life. The fateful day, 12 November 1985, was scorched in my heart and Jenny's last words rang in my ears all the time. Yet, sitting on the porch and looking at nature and children playing around made my loss appear unreal.

With time, my heart still ached with sorrow but it was no longer the raw searing pain of a fresh wound, as if a callus had formed. I often felt guilty I hadn't thought of her for some time till it became painfully true that somehow, unknowingly, I had adjusted to life without dear Jenny, comforted in the thought that I would soon join her.

One day Madan brought me a faded black-and-white photograph of a younger me sitting on an elephant with Baoji. 'Grandpa, Dad says this child is you, but he wasn't sure who this man is.'

'Son, that's my Dad, Baoji. I was around ten years old then and this boy by my side is my brother, Bhai.' Even as Madan wandered off I began wishing he knew more about my roots and his; it was tragic that after me the connection would be broken forever. Determined that I owed it to Baoji, Ma, Bhai and even to myself that the two ends of my family, here and in Ambala, remained in touch, I resolved to contact Saket.

Just then Sarah walked into the room. 'I wish you didn't see these old photos all the time. They only make you sad. We must forget the past and move on.'

'It's important for everyone to know their roots. I am sure Madan will love to meet his family in India.'

'Are you serious, Dad? Who in India knows us? I mean, we have relatives but that means nothing. I am sure if we ever crossed paths it would just be as strangers.'

'I disagree. When two people related by blood meet there will be an instant connection. They may not even realize it at that moment, but trust me a bond will be established. I am convinced families bound by ties of blood and love can never separate.'

Sarah quietly digested my words before gently saying, 'Dad, maybe you should speak to your nephew.'

'You are right, dear. That is exactly what I will do.'

But I never did get around to speaking to Saket, though God knows I tried. I then thought I would write to him but I just couldn't bear to write another name in place of Bhai's;

there were many half-written letters I crumpled and threw away.

The wheels of time moved on. News of home trickled in through friends and relatives, but there was no regular contact. Every time I remembered Baoji's endeavor to keep his family together, it saddened me to realize that I had failed him.

And then out of the blue I got news that brought me true happiness after what seemed like ages. Saket called from New York to say he was coming over to spend a weekend. Having him over felt like Bhai was with me and seeing him bond with Sanjay and Madan reassured me I had not failed Baoji and Ma.

Glendale, Ontario: 1991

Sanjay and Riya tenderly held Uncle's hand as he took a short breath, exhaled ever so softly and became perfectly still. Grief stricken, Sanjay looked at me and softly said, 'Dad's gone, Saket' and closed his eyes. Everyone was crying. I respectfully touched his feet and left wordlessly after hugging Sanjay tightly. I knew what I had to do.

I entered the basement with leaden steps, beckoned by a fading poster paper—Uncle's wall of remembrance—bearing testimony to the memories of his loved ones. With shaking hands, I took his photograph from my pocket, pasted it in the blank space beside my father's photo and completed the inscription, 'Rohan Lal—1900 (Ambala) to 1991 (Glendale)'. Then I paid homage to my ancestors.

It was all too familiar an event, but remarkable for its strange setting; a Harvard-educated pandit chanting mantras from the Gita, the holy book of Hindus, in modern day Glendale for an audience that largely understood not a single word. Sanjay, Riya, Sarah, Madan and his wife, Laurel, looked vulnerable yet gave each other strength to carry out their appointed tasks as Uncle was cremated. Dressed for the part in a white kurta pajama, Sanjay followed the instructions of the saffron-clad pandit, often turning to me for guidance. The cremation over, we returned home physically and emotionally drained. All that was left to do was pick up and immerse into the holy Ganges to set the soul on its final journey.

Early next morning, Sanjay and I reached the crematorium and were handed a metal urn containing Uncle's ashes. We sat quietly in the car with Sanjay holding the urn that now represented an entire human life. Turning to me he said, 'Dad once told me that on each marriage anniversary Mom made him promise to never leave her alone and after she passed on he renewed his commitment whenever he visited her grave. I also know his entire life his dearest wish was to return home. How can both be possible?'

The minutes ticked by as we tried to resolve the dilemma. Then Sanjay looked at me and, by unspoken consent, slowly drove out of the parking lot. It was a short ride to the cemetery and he led me to a white marble headstone marked simply: 'Jenny Lal'.

A soft breeze blew as Sanjay carefully removed a few weeds and we knelt to pray for the souls of our loved ones. Our prayers done, I opened the urn and Sanjay took some ashes and I did the same. Then, gently closing the urn, we sprinkled the ashes making sure they became one with the grave.

Uncle Rohan and Aunt Jenny now lay forever together in the land they had made their home while they lived and loved. Uncle was keeping his promise to never leave Aunt Jenny. And when his ashes reached India, he would fulfill his promise to return home to Baoji, Ma and Bhai.

Back at Uncle's home I felt restless beyond comprehension; Uncle's passing had changed my world too. Ever since I was a kid, I knew his house through his letters and remembered my thrill on first visiting him a few years back. As we spoke in our native language, he had tenderly brushed aside Sanjay who felt left out. 'No son, don't stop me now. It has been so long since I heard and spoke this most wonderful language of all.' Then turning to me he had said, 'The greatest loss for a man is to lose his roots...by settling here I lost my language, food, culture, everything.' It had saddened me then. I was still uncertain if he was finally at peace now.

It was time to leave and over breakfast Sanjay and I promised to stay in touch. 'Sanjay, I will be in New York for some time before returning home. I have few years of service left and will settle in Ambala. I hope you will visit. My home will always be yours just as it was Uncle's.'

'Yes, we will have a prayer meeting for Dad there. You know, as a child I was especially sensitive to Dad's longing for his birthplace but am thankful that he stayed here for us. So I tried to make him happy by learning his language, cooking his food, and even giving my child an Indian name. I tried that he did not miss his old life, but I am not sure I succeeded.'

'Well, Uncle had finally accepted his destiny.'

'Yes, he once told me he had gradually understood what his Baoji meant when he said man's greatest misfortune is to die away from his birthplace. It simply meant it was a tragedy to face one's maker alone without family and friends and he had no such fear since we were with him. I am glad he will always be with us for all time to come and will also return home with you. In his death he is fulfilling a promise he could not keep when alive.' '

As I nodded in agreement, Sanjay got up. 'Come, I want to give you something.'

He led me to the basement and immediately noticed the change on the poster paper. 'I guess you added Dad's photo?'

'Yes, Uncle had asked me to do so.'

'Dad used to spend hours praying before these photos. Anyway, I found this packet in his papers.'

Sanjay took out a bulky brown packet from a drawer. He opened it carefully, took out a few letters and handed them to me.

'These are your dad's letters that I can't read since I don't know the language. I would like you to keep these. No one here can read them and these meant a lot to Dad. It is fitting these be with you. By the way, you notice these are addressed to "Prince Rohan"? I remember once asking Dad and he just smiled and said it was a private joke with his Bhai.'

My thoughts instantly went back to all the times I would find Dad in his study writing to Uncle; they had been in correspondence for over half a century. Opening one of the yellowed, fragile letters, I understood why Sanjay could not read them—they were in Urdu—the language of the educated class in undivided Punjab. Being slightly familiar with the language, I read out a few lines to Sanjay.

It did seem I was the natural inheritor of the correspondence Uncle treasured so deeply. 'Even Dad kept all of Uncle's letters so I will now keep their letters together. Through them our children and grandchildren will appreciate the thoughts and sentiments of their forefathers.'

As we turned to leave, my eyes fell again on the poster paper and I spontaneously asked, 'Sanjay, I wonder if I could have this too?'

He hesitated before lovingly taking down the poster paper, his eyes teary as if he was once again saying goodbye to Uncle. 'Sure, Dad always wanted to be with his family and I will think this way his wish is being fulfilled. I have so many photos, but these are special and should be at his home in India.'

I looked back just before exiting the basement. At that moment, I could have sworn Uncle was at his desk reading Bhai's letter and waving to me, a wide smile on his handsome face.

Sanjay placed my bag in the car, and I kept the urn, packet of letters, and poster paper on the passenger seat and slowly reversed out of the driveway, looking one last time at Uncle's house as my family waved goodbye. As I turned away, my last thought was how closely Madan resembled Dad.

It was a bright day and it felt good to be on the road; Uncle was no more yet I was taking him home and my spirits were uplifted. When the Customs Officer at the Thousand Island Bridge courteously asked if I had anything to declare, I briefly glanced at the passenger seat and replied, 'A lifetime of memories'.

Haridwar, Uttar Pradesh: 1991

Immersion of ashes in the Ganga at Haridwar, the gateway to God, is believed to take the soul directly to the Supreme One. Manoj and I checked into a dharamshala, the same one that I had stayed in when Mom had passed on, and while I preferred to rest, he was drawn by the ringing bells of the bustling temple town inviting worshipers for the evening aarti at Har-Ki-Pauri, the sacred ghat.

I placed the urn with Uncle's ashes on a side table. The sounds of the marketplace, the chants of pandits, the temple bells, all mixed together in a soothing balm, making it comforting to be in the land of the living yet so near the faithful's doorway to heaven; somehow this seemed to demystify death. A cool breeze wafted in through an open window and I lay on my bed looking at the twinkling lights below me, till I eventually dozed off.

I awoke to the sound of ringing bells and early morning prayers. Dawn was breaking over the city as I bathed and then woke Manoj.

'Dad, mind if I ask something?' Manoj said when he was ready. 'Why has no one come from Canada? Isn't it essential for a son to perform these last rites.'

'Uncle was your grandfather's brother, so he was like my

father too. Sanjay wanted to come, but I told him the scriptures allow me to do the ceremony. Come, let's hurry.'

Manoj picked up our bag of clothes and the customary gifts and sweets for the pandit while I took the urn...not simply cold ash but the sum and substance of an entire life—infant, child, youth, adult, son, brother, husband, father, grandfather. And all the lives that are lived in between and beyond these labels.

Descending the narrow stairs, we walked to the riverbank where all the pandits lived; record keepers of each family's births and deaths over generations. I remembered the way from my last visit and we soon stood in front of Vishnu Prasad Pandit's house. The door was open and a little girl came out to direct us to the riverbank. Making our way to the indicated spot, I immediately spotted Vishnu Prasad, tonsuring a small boy. Around us people were busy in rituals; some marking the birth of a child, others performing the last rites of someone they had lost.

We waited patiently till Vishnu Prasad was with us; the urn I held told him why he were there. Taking a thick register from his sling bag, he asked my family name and turned to the particular page that listed my forefathers going back over a hundred years. Business-like, he asked the date and place of Uncle's death and noted them down. It was now recorded for posterity that Rohan Lal, born in Ambala, India in 1900, had died in Glendale, Canada at the age of ninety-one.

Our pandit began the rituals and with the Ganga flowing at our feet, we prayed to the gods to grant peace to Uncle's soul. Then, as the sun rose, he asked me to lift the urn and slowly release the ashes.

I watched as the grey dust scattered in the wind, sparkling

briefly upon catching the golden sun rays before falling, as if in slow motion, into the cool, eternal river, momentarily resting on the blue blanket before being completely absorbed in the swirling, rushing water, no more to be seen, carried away, no doubt, to heaven where dear Uncle's soul would be welcomed by his family. He had left his land and loved ones long ago and spent his entire life keeping their memory alive, and now he had finally returned home, never to leave.

I did not visit Canada again. I spoke with Sanjay a couple times but lost contact with him eventually, though I often thought of him and Uncle Rohan. Time and again I found myself drawn to Dad's and Uncle's letters. Uncle's life-long dilemma disturbed me and I often recalled a conversation when he said, 'Each moment I pray that by living abroad I did not commit the sin of breaking my family so that when I die, I can face Baoji, Ma and Bhai without shame.'

EPILOGUE

Heathrow Airport, London: 2040

'Flight 023 to Ottawa is delayed; boarding will commence at 18:30 hours from Gate 43. Inconvenience is regretted.'

Sammy observed the milling passengers with amusement when his eyes locked briefly with a man only slightly older than him, but the moment passed. After a few minutes he walked over and placed a $10 bill on the coffee counter. 'One Cappuccino, please.'

Picking his coffee, he turned to find himself face to face with the same man, who was pointing to the sales girl holding coins in her outstretched hand. 'You forgot the change.'

'Shucks! Thanks.'

For some inexplicable reason, Sammy waited for him to get his coffee and asked, 'You traveling to Ottawa?'

'No, to Ambala in India.'

'Oh, I thought only Ottawa passengers were here.'

'So, are *you* going to Ottawa?'

'Yes, I am. By the way, I am Sammy.' They shook hands.

'Nice to meet you. I am Rishi.'

Walking towards a few empty chairs, Sammy wondered why he felt pulled to talk to this stranger. 'Is your flight delayed too?'

'Only by an hour. And yours?'

'They announced a 18:30 departure, but you never know. I hope it's not further delayed otherwise I'll reach home very late at night.'

'Do you stay far from the airport?'

'About an hour's drive, in Glendale. It's a small town.'

'Why, I know of it! My Grandpa has a bunch of old letters from someone there. God knows who!'

'That's interesting. I don't mean to pry, but what do you do? I would put you down as a tech guy.'

'Ha! Ha! If only my Dad had heard you. You see, and I don't mind sharing this, he tries so hard to make me join him in IT.'

'That's my field, what's his name?'

'Bharat, and he runs Indesque Automation.'

'No way! Huge fan!'

'He is an AI expert. But I fancy myself as a writer. In fact, I just attended the Euro-Writers' Conference.'

A stuffed toy hit Sammy's hand, causing his coffee to spill. 'Whew! What was that?' he exclaimed, standing to survey the damage to his suit.

'Better wash it, coffee stains are stubborn,' Rishi advised sympathetically. 'Well, I see my flight's boarding. Here's my card, do call if you visit India.'

'Thanks,' replied Sammy, slipping the card into his pocket while continuing to dry himself. 'Here's mine. It was a pleasure meeting you. Have a nice flight.'

'You too,' said Rishi, quickly pocketing the card and moving towards the boarding gate; he considered traveling first class 'un-writer-like' but permitted himself the luxury, thanks to his dad's indulgence.

'Welcome, Sir,' said the airline agent with a warm smile. Just as he crossed her, she asked, 'And your brother, Sir?'

'My brother?' Rishi paused in his stride.

'I am sorry, Sir. I thought the person you were with was your brother. You look so much alike.'

'No, no you are mistaken, that was just someone I met for the first time.'